Out Of Her Dreams

"Can I buy you a drink?" he asked smoothly. He looked over at the redhead and noticed that her hands were shaking and she was very pale. He wondered what was wrong with her.

Connie couldn't believe she was hearing the voice that'd haunted her dreams for the last month. His voice was low and rough, at odds with his dark good looks. Her hands were shaking and she clasped them together in her lap when she noticed him looking at them. She was sure her face was chalk-white. She was cold and her heart was racing in her chest. She kicked Erin under the table and Erin looked over startled.

Erin couldn't believe how pale Connie was. What in the world was wrong? She'd been fine a minute ago. "What's wrong, Connie?" she asked, her voice full of concern.

Connie managed to pull herself together and say, "I'm okay. It's just a headache coming on. We'd better get going while I can still drive. Excuse us please," she said sliding across the seat and exiting the booth.

She brushed quickly past the man, and hurried outside, not even looking to see if Erin was following. She was afraid she was going to be sick. That awful voice was filling her head. She swayed and leaned against the restaurant's wall. A hand on her shoulder startled her, and she looked up apprehensively.

Colleen,

Hold fast to
your dreams but
keep your faith
in God!

Anita

Wings

Out Of Her Dreams

by

Anita Lourcey Tooke

Anita L. Tooke

A Wings ePress, Inc.

Romantic Suspense Novel

Wings ePress, Inc.

Edited by: Anita York
Copy Edited by: Ann Oortman
Senior Editor: Lorraine Stephens
Executive Editor: Lorraine Stephens
Cover Artist: Pam Ripling

All rights reserved

Wings ePress Books
http://www.wings-press.com

Copyright © 2002 by Anita Lourcey Tooke
ISBN 1-59088-891-X

Published In the United States Of America

August 2002

Wings ePress Inc.
403 Wallace Court
Richmond, KY 40475

Dedication

To my beloved husband, Gregory
and our daughter, Constance.
I have been truly, wonderfully blessed
to have you both in my life.

Acknowledgements

I wish to thank the following people for their help on the long road to publication.

Mary Justino, Public Information Consultant for the Clay County Sheriff's Office. Many thanks for taking the time to answer my many questions. I'm sure I'll be calling again.

Carron Tooke, you are a wonderful sister-in-law and a remarkable human being. Thanks for being my friend and my photographer.

Erin Jones, I can barely remember what my life was like before you were my friend. You were a great sounding board and an exceptional cheerleader.

Jean Tooke, every woman should be so blessed to have a mother-in-law like you. Thanks for reading the story and correcting my mistakes.

Jenny Collier, my friend. It's been a long time since fifth grade, but it sure has been fun.

James Tooke, you know you should have been my godson. Thanks for helping with the cover. You are very special to me.

Prologue

When Connie was five, all the monsters in the world hid in the dark of night under her bed and could be frightened away by her father's booming voice. She was twenty-eight now, and she knew that real evil did not bother to hide in the dark. It walked the street beside her and had lunch at the same restaurants she did. Connie had seen evil, and she recognized his voice.

One

Connie sank into the car seat with a sigh. She had enjoyed the party, but right now she was wishing she hadn't stayed quite so late. She was not looking forward to the hour-long drive back into the country. She was tired, and the roads were narrow and dark. It was cool outside, so she opened her window a bit. She drove carefully, giving her full attention to the road.

Forty-five minutes later, she turned onto County Road 358 and gave a sigh of relief. *Almost home now*, she thought. This was the darkest part of the trip, so she turned on her high beams and slowed down to about 30 mph. She would never have seen him otherwise. He was standing near the trees that ran along the side of the road. He looked up, startled, as her high beams caught him in their powerful glare. Connie looked at him as he ran toward the car, shouting. Startled, she pressed harder on the accelerator and sped away from him.

Ten minutes later she unlocked the door of her home. She turned on some lights and checked her answering machine for messages. Later, as she stood under the spray of a hot shower, she thought about the man she had seen. She guessed he must have wanted a ride somewhere. Unfortunately for him she didn't pick up strangers for any reason. She hoped he'd gotten wherever he was going safely. She slipped into bed a few minutes later and fell off to sleep at once.

Connie awakened the next morning to the sound of rain pounding on the tin roof of her house. She grimaced as she looked out of the window at the soggy world outside. It was Sunday, and she would have to go out in this messy weather to get to Mass. A devout Roman Catholic, she never missed Mass unless she was too ill to attend. She showered and washed her hair quickly. Dressed in a slim black skirt and sweater, she applied her makeup and stepped into her shoes. She hurried out to her car and slipped behind the wheel wishing, as she shook the raindrops from her hair, that she had a garage. Unfortunately these old farmhouses just didn't look right with attached garages.

Connie's house had belonged to her grandparents. As the only child of two only children, she had inherited the place when her parents were killed in an auto accident the previous year. With the money from the insurance policies and her teacher's salary, she was able to live very comfortably. She started the engine and drove off to church. Our Lady of the Holy Rosary was only about twenty minutes away from here.

On CR 358, near the spot where she had seen the man the previous night, Connie slowed her car and looked off into the woods. She was able to see very little due to the inclement weather. As she peered out of the car window, she spotted something white lying just past the tree line. She stopped the car and opened her window for a better look. To her horror she realized that it was a body. Too frightened to leave the safety of her car, she reached for her cell phone and quickly dialed 911. Almost incoherent, she answered the questions of the operator. She was told that an officer had been dispatched and was asked to wait in her car until he arrived. *Surely she didn't think I was getting out my car*, thought Connie.

She waited for what seemed like hours, but was really only about ten minutes until the officer arrived. He pulled off the side of the road and, leaving his lights on, got out of the car. As he approached her, she could see that he was on his radio and looking around the area. Spotting the body, she heard him call for rescue and for backup. He motioned for her to stay in her car, then jumped over the ditch and ran to the body. He bent down, and she could see that he was checking for a pulse and heartbeat. He stood up and looked around the area. From her vantage point in the car, Connie watched as he surveyed the site. He was talking into his radio again and she assumed because he had not begun CPR that whoever was lying there was beyond help. She began to cry.

When Lieutenant Greg Reed received the call from dispatch, he was just starting his morning shift. The rain came down fast and furiously as he drove the five or so miles to the site. Pulling over, he spotted the late-model black Ford Mustang on the shoulder of the road. He motioned for the young woman to stay in her car and began to look around. *Probably nothing more than a bag of garbage that someone had thrown from their car*, he thought. As he got closer, he realized that it was indeed a body. Looking down, he knew from his training that it was too late for medical help, but he had to check for vital signs anyway. There was no pulse and no heartbeat.

The body was that of a young female, probably in her late twenties. He could see that she had been stabbed numerous times and that the wounds appeared to be deep. Looking around the site he noticed that the ground appeared to be disturbed as if something had been dragged over it.

He called dispatch and asked them to send the forensics team. Careful not to disturb the ground, he made his way back to the young woman in the car. She opened her window as he approached. "I'm Lieutenant Greg Reed," he said. She

3

introduced herself as Connie Mitchell and produced her driver's license when he asked for some ID. She was twenty-eight according to her license, although he thought she looked younger. "Would you like to wait in my car until the other officers get here?" he inquired.

She nodded her head gratefully, and he opened the door. She stepped out, and he followed her to the patrol car. He noticed that she was petite, the top of her head coming only to his shoulder when they were standing. She slid in gracefully as he held the door open. He could hear the sirens as the other officers approached the scene. He closed the door and left her in the car.

Deputies' Crawford and Cook pulled up and came toward him. "What have we got here?" Mike Cook asked. As Greg briefed the two officers, the forensic team pulled up. He directed them to the body, and they began the task of gathering evidence. Returning to his car, he told Connie that she would need to come down to the station and give her statement. He offered to drive her there and she accepted. She seemed small and frightened. She probably wasn't accustomed to finding dead bodies on the side of the road.

Connie was scared, and she felt more than a little nauseous during the trip to the station. Lieutenant Reed was kind and solicitous as he ushered her into his office.

"Would you like a cup of coffee?" he asked.

Connie was not normally a coffee drinker, but she accepted. Maybe it would help remove the chill that seemed to have settled in her bones. As she gave her statement to the lieutenant, she assumed that the body was that of the man she had seen on Saturday night, so she was surprised and shocked to learn that the victim was a female. "But it was a man I saw last night!" she exclaimed. Connie described what she had seen the night before, and he listened in stunned silence.

Greg couldn't believe what he was hearing. Didn't she realize that she might have seen the murderer? As he questioned her further, he could tell by the look on her face when the thought occurred to her as well. She went pale as death, and her eyes grew wide with shock.

Two

Connie sat in silence as Lieutenant Reed drove her back to her car. He had taken the remainder of her statement and then given her a copy to sign. She could see that he was perturbed by what she had seen the previous night. To be honest, she felt exactly the same way.

She also felt somewhat sad and not a little guilty. She wondered if she might have been able to save this woman if only she had paid more attention to what had been going on instead of hurrying away as she had.

As they arrived at the spot where she had left her car, she averted her eyes from the bright yellow tape that marked the crime scene. She hurried to her car, scarcely noticing that Lieutenant Reed was watching her with concern.

"Miss Mitchell," he said, "I'll be happy to follow you home if you like."

"No thank you," Connie said. "I'm sure I'll be fine." She got in the car and hurriedly left.

Greg watched as she drove away from the scene. He knew that she was extremely upset by everything that had occurred. He had done his best to reassure her that she couldn't have done anything to change the situation. Indeed, she herself might have become the victim if she had reacted differently. He crossed over to the crime scene and stepped over the tape surrounding the area. The forensic team had finished here about an hour before, but still he was careful not to disturb anything. Even though the rain had been heavy during the early morning hours, he could still see signs of the body having been dragged to this spot. It was late fall and the leaves lay heavy on the ground. Even the heavy rain of the previous night hadn't wiped away the evidence. The question was had the killer dragged her here or had she been trying to get away and pulled herself along to, this point? The pathologist might be able to answer that question for him. He returned to his car and went back to the station to confer with the others working on this case.

Connie drove home quickly. She couldn't wait to be safely behind her locked doors. She had been at the station for almost five hours, and it was now 5:30 p.m.

The days were short this time of year, and dusk was tinting the sky a beautiful smoky blue. She hurried up the steps to the door and let herself in the house. Bolting the door behind her, she turned on all the lights and made herself a cup of hot tea. Although it wasn't all that cold outside, she lit the fire in the fireplace and turned on the central heat as well. She was cold! As cold as death!

She snuggled under a blanket on the couch by the fire and tried not to think of the happenings of the day. But try as she might she was unable to get the rid of the mental pictures of the dead woman and the man that she had seen. She got up, went into the kitchen, and heated up some homemade vegetable soup, then made herself a cheese sandwich. She ate her meal in front of the TV, although later she had no memory of what she had watched.

By nine, she was exhausted and ready for bed. Since she knew she would probably have trouble sleeping, she took two of the pills the doctor had prescribed for her when her parents had been killed. Even with the pills, she slept fretfully and awoke just before 6 a.m.

She arose and showered as she always did and dressed for work. She had her morning cup of tea on the porch and listened to the birds singing. There was always something about this old place that made her happy to be alive. This morning was no different.

The morning sun was just poking its head above the trees. It turned their remaining leaves into molten gold. She loved this time of the year. It was cool but not cold; the morning low had been about fifty degrees. It would warm up into the lower seventies by early afternoon. At 7:30, she left for work.

The drive into town took her by the crime scene once more. She was not surprised to see that there were police cars there again. She supposed that it would take a great deal of time to completely go over the scene. She passed quickly by and continued on her way.

She arrived at the school where she had been teaching for six years at 8:15, and threw herself into her usual routine. When the last bell rang at 3:30, she was relieved. She had been hard-pressed to concentrate on what she needed to do and her third-grade students, having taken notice of this, had been unusually unruly.

She stopped at the local supermarket on her way home. She needed food and cleaning supplies. On her way out, she purchased a newspaper from the stand. She wanted to see if the body had been identified yet.

The murder was front-page news. She scanned the article looking for information. All the technical aspects of the murder were listed, and the crime scene was described in great detail, but there was actually very little information about the victim. General facts such as height, weight, hair color, clothing, and build were included, but little else. Her identity was being withheld, pending notification of her next of kin. Disappointed, Connie drove home, once more passing the crime scene. As she pulled into her driveway she was surprised to see Lieutenant Reed lounging in one of the rockers on her porch. He stood up as she got out of the car.

"Good afternoon," he said. "Would you like some help with those bags?"

"Hello," Connie said hesitantly, wondering why he was here. She accepted his help with the groceries, and he followed her into the kitchen.

"Great place you've got here," he said.

Looking around, Connie nodded. She continued putting things away, waiting for him to explain his presence.

Greg was silent as he watched Connie. He wasn't really sure why he was here, he had just felt the urge to see her and make sure she was all right. She had been in shock yesterday, and he had been concerned about her since then. He had been tempted to call several times last night, but wasn't sure she would have appreciated that. He looked around the place as he tried to gather his thoughts. *This really is a beautiful old house,* he thought.

The front door opened into a large room about 30 feet by 30 feet that was both living and dining room. The kitchen was off to the right, and a short hallway led off to the left. The floors were knotty pine, as were the walls in the living/dining room. A round oak table with eight chairs dominated the dining room. An oak buffet sat against the wall on one side and an oak hutch on the other. The living room was beautiful and charming with its great brick fireplace and comfortable sofa and chairs. Marble-topped tables and an upright piano added to its charm. There were candles in both rooms, and he could see that she used them. She must like burgundy and green, as these were the main colors in the two rooms.

The walls of the kitchen were lined with cabinets with glass fronts, and the counter tops were tile. As in the other room, large windows hung with lace curtains allowed the late afternoon sunshine to flood the room. A smaller table sat in the center of the kitchen. Fall flowers filled the vase on the table. The whole effect was warm and inviting. He loved it.

He turned back to watch Connie. *She's beautiful*, he thought. Her skin glowed with good health; her amber eyes had wonderful golden flecks in them. Her figure was curvy in all the right places. The afternoon sun danced on the highlights in her auburn hair as she reached into the upper cabinets. He became aware the Connie had finished her stowing of the groceries and was now watching him with a curious look on her face.

"Would you like a glass of juice or a cup of tea?" she asked. She was avoiding asking why he was there.

"A glass of water would be nice," he said.

She took down a glass, filled it with water, and handed it to him. She put water on for tea and then motioned for him to sit. She seated herself across from him and finally asked, "Is there something more that you need from me?" She watched his face as he struggled to answer her question.

Greg couldn't seem to find the right words. Finally he said, "I was worried about you and I wanted to make sure that you were okay. I could see that you were terribly upset yesterday."

Connie was surprised by his words, but strangely comforted as well. She had been feeling out of sorts all day and really needed to know that someone cared. It was very lonely having no family to confide in at times. She had plenty of friends, but had not called any of them as yet. As if on cue the phone rang. "Excuse me," she said picking up the phone. "Hello. Oh, hi Erin. What's up?" She listened for a few minutes and then said, "I'll call you back later and let you know." Replacing the receiver, she turned back to Lieutenant Reed. "I really appreciate your concern. I'm fine, but I would like to know if you've learned anything new about the woman."

"We're waiting for the autopsy report so that we can get an exact time of death. The rain washed away much of the evidence, but we're hoping to get some leads once her family comes forth. We would like you to come down to the station and go through some photos to see if you can identify the man you saw," he said.

"But it was so dark, and I only saw him for a moment," Connie said. "I could probably recognize his voice easier than I could his face." Lieutenant Reed looked surprised, and she hastened to explain. "I teach school, third grade, and we play this voice recognition game. We close our eyes and listen to each other read or talk and try to recognize the voice. I try to teach the kids not to rely on just their visual sense, but to develop their other senses as well. We do a lot of the listening exercises because the kids really enjoy them."

"Well, we'd really like you to try a visual program that we have on the computer at the station. It's very easy to use, and the technician will lead you through it step by step. We've had good results in the past with this method. Unlike a sketch artist, this is much faster and allows for a greater variety of facial characteristics. We'd like to set up the appointment for tomorrow afternoon if that's possible," Greg said.

"I'm usually done at school by four," Connie said. "Anytime after that would be fine. I'll do my best, but I can't promise you how good that's going to be."

Greg stood up to leave. He told Connie that he would meet her the following afternoon at the station around 4:15. Connie walked with him outside and down the steps to his car. As he drove away, he was aware that she watched him until he was out of sight.

When she could no longer see his car, Connie turned and went back into the house. She had some calls to make and she needed to get ready for choir practice. She'd better call Erin. She lived only a few miles up the road, and they usually drove together to practice.

She answered on the first ring. *Geeze,* Connie thought, *she must have been sitting there waiting for it to ring.*

Erin Sims was a very close friend. They had grown up together, and she had been like a sister to Connie. They liked the same things and the same people and rarely disagreed over anything. Erin was bright and vivacious. She was caring and unselfish and had a great many friends. Like Connie, Erin was single. Neither had met a man they wanted to spend the rest of their lives with as of yet. Because they were both Catholic, they dated carefully and didn't waste time with men who only were interested in having a good time. They liked having a good time themselves, but they didn't encourage men they knew they could never marry.

Erin was the Head Librarian at the public library. She was good at her job and loved it. She was always telling Connie, "One day I'm going to write a book and be famous." Connie always laughed. The very idea of Erin sitting in front of a computer long enough to write a book was inconceivable. She was always so busy; she never seemed to have time to sit still for more than ten minutes. She did volunteer work at the school, helped at church, and visited people at the nursing home in town. She was rarely home, except to sleep. Connie loved her.

"Hey!" Erin said as she answered the phone. "What was that good looking police officer doing at your house this afternoon? I saw him sitting on the porch on my way home."

Connie had been told by the police not to mention what she had seen. She didn't want to lie to Erin, so she searched her brain frantically for something to say. "He was talking to people in the area about the murder," she said. "He wanted to know if I had seen anything suspicious recently."

"Wasn't that just awful!" Erin exclaimed. "We always think nothing like that will ever happen around here. The paper didn't give her name. I wonder who she was?"

"I don't know," Connie said. "The officer was looking for information, not giving it out."

Hurt, Erin replied. "You don't have to sound so nasty, Connie. I was just curious."

"I'm sorry, Erin. I've had a rough day at school. I didn't mean to take it out on you."

This wasn't really a lie, just not the whole truth.

"No problem," Erin said. "Are you feeling all right? I missed you at Mass yesterday."

"I'm fine," Connie replied, "just a little under the weather."

"Are you going to practice tonight?" Erin asked.

"Yes," said Connie. "How about picking me up around 6:45?"

"Okay," Erin said. "See you then."

Connie said good-bye and then made a few other calls. She called the carpenter who had done some work after she had moved into the house. The front door was sticking, and it was hard to close, especially when it was raining. It had been wetter than normal this year, and Connie wanted to get it fixed. Keith Thomas assured her that he would be by to look at the door as soon as possible. He was a good carpenter and stayed very busy. Connie hung up and prepared some dinner.

While dinner was cooking, she changed into a pair of jeans, a chunky white sweater, and tennis shoes.

At 6:45, Erin arrived and they left for practice. Erin was a careful driver, though a bit too fast for Connie's taste. They chatted about their respective days at work for a few minutes, and then Erin once again asked Connie about Lieutenant Reed.

"So what did you think of our city's finest?" she asked.

"He was very nice," Connie replied, "and very considerate."

"Quite good looking, too," Erin said.

Connie sat quietly for a moment, thinking about Lieutenant Reed. He was good-looking in an earthy way. He was about six feet three inches tall, broad-shouldered, with sparkling brown eyes and sable brown hair that just brushed the collar of his shirt in the back. He looked strong and capable. She had to admit that something about him intrigued her. Finally she said, "Yes, he is nice looking, and I wouldn't mind getting to know him better."

Erin laughed knowingly, "Maybe he can introduce me to one of his fellow officers."

Our Lady of the Holy Rosary was a small parish of 200 families. The church itself was small. Built at the turn of the century, it was very traditional in its appearance. The structure was wood-framed and painted white with red trim. The bell tower rose high into the air among the many trees that surrounded the church. Behind the building was the cemetery. Erin parked the car, and the two women went inside.

The church was dimly lighted and smelled faintly of incense. Large stained-glass windows worked in brilliant colors reached almost to the ceiling. Wooden floors gleamed with a soft patina. The pews were wooden with attached kneelers. Statues of Mary and Joseph stood in one wing. The other wing was where the choir sat. A red candle burned over the tabernacle at the front of the church.

The altar was high and white and carved with intricate detail. A picture of the *Last Supper* had been carved into the bottom of the altar. A newer, smaller altar stood in front, as the priest was no longer allowed to have his back to the congregation during Mass.

They were greeted by other members of the choir and were soon engrossed in practice. Thirty minutes later, choir director Russell Williams called for the soloists to come forward to practice their parts. Connie always hated this part of practice. Although she had been blessed with a beautiful voice, she did not feel comfortable singing solo. Still, it was her way of giving back to God, thanking him for her many blessings. She was the first to sing, and she was glad to be done.

She returned to her seat, and Russell called for Eleanor Lincoln. Connie was surprised when she failed to appear. Eleanor was the same age as Connie and Erin. She had moved to Rosemount the previous year and was very active in the community, especially the church. She rarely missed practice.

"Has anyone heard from Eleanor today?" Russ asked.

No one had, and several people recalled that she had not been at Mass on Sunday either.

"Maybe she has that same bug that you do," Erin said to Connie.

Connie shrugged and looked away from her. Sometimes Erin was just too astute. Connie had a sick feeling in the pit of her stomach that had nothing to do with what she had eaten for dinner. She remembered the body alongside the road and the general description given in the newspaper. It fit Eleanor. *Dear God*, she prayed, *please don't let it be Eleanor.*

Eleanor was a friend. They had met when she started attending Mass and liked each other instantly. Eleanor was quiet like Connie. But, unlike Connie, she dated anyone who asked. She seemed almost desperate in her search for a husband. Connie knew she was lonely and had made every effort to include her in activities.

Eleanor was well-liked. She was an attractive woman, about 5-feet, 5-inches tall. She had wavy black hair that fell almost to her waist. She was thin, almost too thin. She dressed well, and men seemed to like her. Connie had warned her about several of the men she had dated, but Eleanor had only shrugged. *I'd better call and check on her when I get home*, Connie thought.

Practice ended and everyone milled around chatting for a short time. The main topic of conversation was the murder. Rosemount was a small town with little crime. No one could recall any murders for the past twenty years or more. Connie and Erin left shortly after nine. They were quiet for most of the ride home.

When Erin turned onto CR 358, Connie was startled. They usually went the back way to and from practice because it was not as dark. "Hey," Connie said, "What are you doing?"

"I want to see where they found the body," Erin answered.

"That's really gruesome," Connie said.

"Oh well, you know me," Erin said cheerfully. "You know how I love a good mystery."

Connie supposed Erin hadn't for one second thought that Eleanor might be the victim. If she had, she wouldn't be so blasé about seeing the crime scene. Erin slowed the car when she spotted the yellow tape. To Connie's dismay, she pulled off the road.

"What in the world are you thinking?" Connie asked.

"I just want to get a closer look," Erin said.

"Erin, please, let's go home," Connie pleaded.

Erin took in Connie's pale face and nodded. "I guess it is pretty gruesome after all," she said.

When she dropped Connie off at home a few minutes later, she gave her a hug. "Buck up gal. Tomorrow will be a better day." Connie hugged her back and said goodnight.

Once inside she headed straight for the phone. She dialed Eleanor's number quickly and waited anxiously for her to pick up. After the fourth ring, the answering machine took the call. Eleanor's voice was cheerful as she advised her callers that she wasn't home, but would return their calls later. After leaving a short message, Connie hung up. Later, lying in bed, she prayed her Rosary and offered special prayers for Eleanor. She slept fitfully, her rest disturbed by terrible dreams. She was walking down a long corridor and someone was calling her name. She kept trying to run, but couldn't seem to get away from the voice. Connie woke drenched in sweat and sobbing. Although it was only 4:30 a.m., she knew she would never be able to go back to sleep. She got up and started her morning ritual.

She left for work early and took the long way into town, avoiding CR 358. Later that afternoon, she was tired as she headed over to the police station for her appointment with Lieutenant Reed. She was looking forward to seeing him again, but was dreading the task before her.

Greg met her in the foyer of the police station. He thought she looked beautiful, but tired. She answered his greeting with a small smile. He led her down the hallway to the technician's office. The technician would help her create a composite of the suspect. For the next hour, Greg watched as Connie worked, trying her best to give them a picture of the man she had seen.

At the end of the session, Connie looked at the picture the technician printed out and shook her head helplessly. "He could be anyone," she said. "He looks like the guy at the supermarket, the man who fixes my car, and a guy I dated last year. I warned you that this would happen. I just didn't get a good look at him."

"It's okay, Connie," Greg reassured her, "You did a fine job. At least now we have a general description to go by. Later, you may remember something more that will help us narrow our search."

Connie looked up surprised when he called her by her given name. She had been thinking of him as Greg since yesterday afternoon, but was still bemused by the fact that he evidently thought of her in the same way.

Greg could see the surprise in her face at his use of her Christian name. He couldn't help it. She had become Connie to him that very first day at the station, when she had sat so stoically and given her statement. To him ,she was a very brave woman. Many people chose not to get involved these days. They isolated themselves from their neighbors, behind closed doors and barred windows.

Rosemount was a tight-knit community, and the people here were different. Here you knew your neighbors and helped them when they were in need. That was why everyone was so shocked by this homicide. Most of the townspeople were still unaware of the identity of the victim. Greg had just been given permission to release the name to Connie that afternoon.

He dreaded giving Connie the information because the deceased had been a friend of hers. He knew he had to tell her, though, because the name would appear in the paper tomorrow. He stood and motioned for her to follow him into his office. He seated her and offered a cup of coffee, but she declined politely. "Connie, I have some news for you," he said. "We've learned the identity of the victim." He waited tensely for her reaction.

Connie tensed. She was afraid to hear what he was going to tell her. She wanted so badly to leave before he could tell her. She knew it wasn't going to be good news. She had felt the same way a year ago when they had called her to the principal's office to tell her that her parents were dead. She braced herself and looked at Greg.

"Tell me," she whispered.

Three

"Her name was Eleanor Lincoln," Greg said. "I believe you knew her." He jumped up as Connie suddenly slumped forward. He pulled her into his arms and held her as she began to sob.

Deep wracking sobs shook her slight frame. She cried until she was too exhausted to cry anymore. Greg led her to the small sofa over by the wall. Connie sank down into its depths and looked up at Greg. *He looks as tormented as I feel*, she thought. He offered to get her some water. She shook her head.

"Will her name be in the paper tomorrow?" she asked.

"Yes," Greg responded. "Her family is on their way here to claim the body. The coroner will be done with it by tomorrow."

Connie rose. She swayed and then steadied herself. "I need to go home now," she said.

"I have some calls to make. I'm not going to let Erin and the others read it in the paper tomorrow."

Greg hesitated before he spoke. "It would be better if you didn't call anyone," he said.

"But why?" Connie asked.

"We don't know who we're dealing with here. Her murderer could be any of a number of people. It may be someone on your list of people to call."

"I don't believe that," Connie said. "No one who really knew her could have done such a thing."

"Most murders are committed by someone the victim knows," Greg said. "No one knows of your involvement in this case yet, and we'd like to keep it that way, at least for now. Our murderer doesn't know who you are. If you make phone calls before the name appears in the paper, people are going to wonder how you got that information. I know this is hard for you, but this is the best way. We still need you to try and help us find our suspect.

Connie nodded. "I suppose you're right, but I hate it. It will be such a shock to Erin and the others. We all liked Eleanor so well. Whatever I can do to help, I will. I can't forget what I saw, but I don't remember anything definite either."

"Give it time," he said. "Don't try so hard to remember. Memories are funny things. When you least expect it you will remember something. My memory usually returns at about two in the morning. By the time I get up, I will have forgotten again. You should keep paper and pen handy. If you remember anything, no matter how inconsequential it may seem, write it down. Sometimes the smallest details are the ones that give us the edge."

"I'll keep trying," she said.

"I'm going to drive you home now," Greg said. "One of the other officers will drive your car home for you." Connie wanted to be strong and insist that she was okay. She knew she'd be lying, though. The thought of driving home alone was scary. Her knees felt weak, and she wasn't sure how much longer she could even stand up. She acquiesced gratefully.

Greg placed his arm around her shoulders, and they left the office. On the way out, he saw Mike Cook and asked him to drive Connie's car home. The other officer nodded and followed them from the station. Connie handed him her keys and followed Greg to his car. She was expecting to ride in his patrol car, but he led her to a white 1965 Mustang that was parked at the rear of the lot.

Greg grinned when he saw Connie's look of appreciation as she gazed at the car. "This is what I drive when I'm not working," he said. "It was my dad's. He gave it to me when I turned thirty. He said he thought I was old enough for a real car then. He let me drive it a couple of times when I was a teenager. I got my first speeding ticket in this car. Needless to say my dad was not impressed by that."

Connie loved Mustangs, old and new. She had always wanted an older model, but had never found one she liked well enough to buy it. This one was a beauty. She could see that he took good care of his car. She watched as Greg put the top down.

"Do you mind?" he asked.

She shook her head. She loved the feel of the wind through her hair.

"I didn't think you would," he said. "I noticed your own car was a convertible."

He opened the door, and she slid across the seat. The interior of the car was a smoky blue. The carpet looked new, and the seats had obviously been reupholstered. She watched Greg as he started the engine and pulled out of the parking lot. He drove competently and courteously. She supposed he would have to, being a police officer. They talked of trivial issues on the trip home. Neither one seemed to want to discuss the case.

It was dark by the time they pulled into her driveway. She had all but forgotten Officer Cook until he pulled in behind them. He handed Connie her keys and stayed outside as Greg walked her into the farmhouse.

Greg watched Connie carefully as she moved around the house turning on the lights. He could see that she was upset, but he wasn't sure what to say. He didn't think she should be alone tonight. He wanted to offer to stay with her himself, but wasn't sure how she would react. "Connie," he said. "Why don't you call a friend and get someone to stay with you tonight."

"Erin is my closest friend," she said, "but I don't think I could be with her tonight without telling her about Eleanor. I'm not very good at deception, and it wouldn't take her ten minutes to tell that something was wrong."

Greg hesitated for a moment then asked, "Would you like me to stay on the couch tonight?"

Connie glanced up swiftly. She wasn't quite sure how to answer. She didn't want to be alone and calling Erin to come over was a no. She liked Greg. He made her feel safe. She'd known him for just a few days, but already she felt comfortable with him. Her instincts told her that his offer to stay on the couch was genuine. She trusted her instincts. They had kept her out of trouble before. "That would be nice," she said, "if it's not too much trouble?"

"No trouble. I'll let Mike take the car home. He can pick me up in the morning. We both work the same shift. Greg turned and went outside. He informed Mike that he was staying.

Mike didn't look surprised. They had been friends for a long time, and he could see that Greg was falling for this woman. *She must be something pretty special,* he thought. Greg was very perceptive, and he wasn't one to fall for just a pretty face. Mike hoped she was everything that Greg thought she was. He didn't want to see his friend get hurt. He took the keys from Greg, "I'll see you in the morning," he said, and left.

Greg returned to the house. Connie was busy in the kitchen at the stove.

"I hope you like beef stew," she said. "I had some in the freezer. It will be about half an hour before it's ready."

Greg thought she looked wonderful standing there at the stove. She had a grace about her every move. "That will be fine. Could you show me where I can wash up?"

Connie led him down the hallway to the bathroom. "There are fresh towels in the closet, and if you'd like to shower, I can wash your uniform for you. I have some of my dad's things in the guestroom. You look about the same size he was, so I'm sure they will fit."

"A shower would be great," he responded. "Your dad's things will do nicely."

"I'll leave them on the bed in the guest room. It's just across the hall." Connie entered the bedroom. Going to the dresser, she opened the second drawer. She removed a pair of jeans and a cotton shirt. Opening another drawer, she took out socks and some boxers. She laid them on the bed. She looked around the room and sighed.

This had been her parents' room when they were alive. Although they hadn't lived here, they spent a great deal of time at the house. They had loved it as much as she did. She felt the tears well up in her eyes as she thought of all the happy times they had shared. She brushed them away with the back of her hand and turning, left the room.

She returned to the kitchen and made a pan of drop biscuits to eat with the stew. While the biscuits were baking, she set the table and lit some candles around the room. She loved the way the candlelight flickered off the walls, giving them a warm glow. She heard Greg coming down the hall.

He came into the kitchen and sniffed appreciatively. "Dinner will be just a few more minutes," she said. "Would you mind putting some ice in the tea glasses?"

"Not at all," Greg responded. "Sure smells good in here." He stepped to the refrigerator and opened the freezer. "Reminds me of being at home when I was a kid. Mom always had something good cooking when I came home from school." He smiled as he took out the ice. Reminiscing about his childhood always made him feel good. "My mom is a great cook. I still like going home for dinner. Sunday dinners are always the best. Her pot roast and fried chicken are my favorites."

Connie smiled and took the biscuits from the oven. She put them in a basket and set it on the table. She dished the stew into two bowls and placed them on the table as Greg put the ice in the glasses.

"Dinner is served," she said. They took their places, and Connie asked if he would like to say the blessing. Greg nodded and blessed the food. "Sounds like you had a great time growing up," she commented.

Greg nodded. "I did. My brothers and sisters and I had a great childhood. Our parents were always there for us, and they still are. We are all very close."

"How many siblings do you have?" Connie asked.

"Two brothers and two sisters," he replied. "I'm the middle child. My brother James is the oldest, then my sister Carron, followed by me, then my brother John, and my sister Patricia. I also have quite a few cousins in this area. We've all stayed pretty close to where we grew up."

Connie looked wistful. "I'm an only child, as were my parents. Growing up, I always pretended Erin was my sister. It must be great to have so many relatives close by. I have plenty of friends, but it's not the same."

Greg had known Connie was an only child. He also knew that her parents were dead. She would probably be surprised to know just how much he knew about her life. He had run a background check on her immediately after she had found the body. She had been ruled out as a suspect when the report came back clean. The forensics report also indicated that it would not have been possible for a woman of her stature to inflict the wounds on the body. The killer had to have been someone powerful. Eleanor had fought hard for her life.

"It's great having them so close," he told her. "We get together often. My brothers and sisters are all married, some with children of their own. We want them to know their cousins. Family is important to us."

Connie nodded agreement. "I miss my parents terribly. We were very close. When they died, I thought I would never get over it. Time really is the great healer, though, and having good friends was a tremendous help to me."

They continued to chat during the remainder of the meal. When they were finished, they cleared the table and loaded the dishes into the dishwasher. She asked for his clothes and put them in the washer.

They settled on the couch in the living room where they watched an old crime show on TV. At ten, Connie announced that she was going to bed. "There are clean linens on the bed in the guest room and an extra toothbrush in the bathroom. I'll put your clothes in the dryer now, and in the morning, I'll fluff them to get the wrinkles out. I get up at 6 a.m. I can wake you then if you'd like."

"That will be fine," he said. She said goodnight, and he watched her go into her room. He wasn't tired yet, so he looked around for a bookcase. Finding one, he selected a book and sat down to read for a while.

It was peaceful. The only sounds were those of the old house settling as the night cooled down and the rhythmic ticking of the grandfather clock in the hallway.

Around midnight, the sound of screaming tore through the quiet. He jumped up and ran down the hall to Connie's room. She was sitting up in bed, still screaming. Her eyes were open, but unseeing. She continued to scream as he crossed quickly to the bed. Greg shook her gently trying to awaken her. She came awake with a start. She looked at him in confusion. He could see that she was trying to figure out what he was doing in her room.

"You must have had a nightmare," he told her. "I heard you screaming. I came in to see what was wrong. You were sitting up in bed screaming."

"I remember now," she said. "I had a terrible dream. Someone was following me down a long hallway, and he kept calling my name. I was running, but I couldn't get away…I'm fine now. It was just a bad dream."

Greg stood up and said goodnight once again. He went into the guestroom and prepared for bed. He left the door open and got into bed. He wanted to be able to hear Connie if she called out again. He could hear her tossing and turning in her room. *She must have given up on going back to sleep,* he thought when he saw the band of light appear under her door. Maybe she was going to read for a while.

Connie wasn't reading. She was praying her Rosary. That always helped when she was upset. She offered this one for Eleanor. She prayed for about half an hour, then she turned off the light and tried to get back to sleep. She kept thinking about how nice it was to have someone else in the house, especially someone like Greg. She liked everything about him so far. She loved the way he smelled—the musky scent of his aftershave—a clean, male smell. She loved the way he looked at her with such concern in his eyes. She thought she was starting to fall in love with him. On this note, she drifted back to sleep with a smile on her face.

When her alarm rang, she got up. Despite the fact that she'd had less sleep than normal she felt great. On her way down the hall, she noticed that the door of the guestroom was open. She smiled to herself. He must have left it open in case she needed him again. She peeked into the room.

In the dawn light, she could see that he was still sleeping. He looked so peaceful that she didn't want to awaken him. As if sensing her presence, he opened his eyes. Connie felt like a naughty schoolgirl caught peeking into the boy's locker room. She should have awakened him immediately, not stood staring at him. "Good morning," she said shyly. "It's time to get up."

Greg looked at Connie. He wasn't sure, but he thought she might be blushing. He had known she was there before he opened his eyes because he could smell the sweet fragrance of her perfume. He hadn't wanted to open his eyes. He just wanted to lie there and inhale the scent of her. She looked wide-awake and refreshed. This surprised him, considering the rough night she'd had. He sat up and said, "Good morning."

As he sat up in bed, the sheet fell away, exposing his upper body to her gaze. She turned away, but not before she had seen his bare chest and arms. His upper arms and chest were well-muscled. She caught just a glimpse of the dark hair on his chest before she averted her eyes. "Would you like some breakfast?" she asked.

"I'll get something in town later," he answered.

"I usually have a cup of tea and some toast, but if you'd like some coffee, I'll put some extra water on to boil," she responded.

Greg nodded and said, "That'll be good. I could use a cup of coffee."

Connie said, "I'll bring your clothes from the dryer in just a few minutes."

"Thank you. I'll just take a quick shower if you don't mind," he said.

"No problem, I'll take mine when you're done. There's not enough water pressure for both showers to be used."

Connie walked through the house and into the laundry room. She set the timer on the dryer for a few minutes to take the wrinkles from his clothes.

Going into the kitchen, she put the water on to boil and sliced some bread from the loaf she had purchased at the bakery on Monday. She set the butter and some blackberry jam on the table, along with two cups. By this time the dryer was finished. She took the clothes out and went back to the bedroom. She could hear water running in the shower, so she laid the clothes on the bed. She was leaving the room when the sound of running water ceased.

Connie went back to her own bathroom and brushed her teeth before stepping into the shower. She was done in about fifteen minutes. She dried her hair and applied some blush and a bit of eye shadow.

She selected a long skirt in a floral print with a creamy yellow background. She topped it with a periwinkle blue sweater that exactly matched some of the flowers on the skirt. Slipping into a pair of winter white pumps, she left her room. She passed his room and noticed that the clothes were gone from the bed. Greg was standing at the window looking out when she entered the kitchen.

"What a great view from this window," he said.

"Yes," she replied. "There is something beautiful to see from every window in the house. I love this place. It belonged to my grandparents. I loved to come here when I was little. It didn't matter what season it was, it was always beautiful to me." She joined him at the window and looked outside.

The morning sun was just peeking its head above the tree line. It golden glow gilded the leaves on the trees in the yard and turned the ones on the ground to molten gold. The birds were feeding just below the window. She turned and put the bread into the toaster. She noticed that he had made her tea and himself a cup of coffee.

"Thanks for making my tea," she said. "Are you sure you wouldn't like a piece of toast?"

Shaking his head, he seated himself at the table. "Are you okay this morning? I know you didn't sleep too well last night."

"I'm fine," she replied. "Thanks for asking and thanks for staying the night. I know I've been a lot of trouble these last few days. I really appreciate all you've done."

"I was glad to be of help," he said. "It hasn't been any trouble at all."

They sat in silence and finished their breakfast. Connie rose and cleared the table. Greg helped her load the dishes. Just as they were finishing up, they heard a car horn.

"That will be Mike," Greg said. Going to the front door, he motioned that he would be out shortly. "Well, I guess I'll see you later," he said. "Call me if you need anything, and I'll let you know if anything new comes up."

Connie nodded and wished him a good day. She watched as he walked to the car and got into it. She waved as they left. Picking up her keys and purse from the table, she left the house, locking the door behind her. She noticed that it was still sticking and made a mental note to call Mr. Thomas again.

As she drove to work, she remembered that Eleanor would be identified in the paper today. That made her remember her dream of the past night. There was something about the voice in her dream. Something she just couldn't put her finger on easily. Maybe it would come to her later. Right now, she needed to concentrate on getting to the school on time.

Four

Of all the women at the club, he had known immediately that she was the one. She had tried so hard to fit into the crowd. She wanted so desperately to please. It had been so easy to convince her to go out with him. She was so eager that she hadn't even questioned him when he suggested meeting in Charlotte, instead of Rosemount. He'd told her it was less complicated that way. He hadn't wanted anyone to see them together. She had been so easy, just like all the others. He'd wined them and dined them, taken them to bed a few times, gotten bored, and move on quickly.

He hadn't planned on Eleanor falling in love. He hadn't even been able to get her into bed. Her antiquated morals kept getting in the way.

When she had started talking about marriage, he knew he had to end it. What he hadn't planned on was that she would be hard to get rid of painlessly. He tried to let her down easy. He told her that he wasn't the marrying kind. She had cried and begged him for a second chance. She promised not to mention marriage again. He hadn't believed her. Eleanor was too eager to continue the relationship. He knew she was hoping he would change his mind. What he hadn't told her was that he was already married. It was unfortunate that she had seen him with his wife so soon after.

He had canceled his date with Eleanor for that evening. He had left a message on her machine, but she hadn't gone home. Instead, she came straight to the restaurant where they usually met, the same restaurant where his wife wanted to have dinner. He had agreed to go so as not to arouse her suspicion.

He knew his wife was beginning to suspect him of cheating. If he hadn't signed that prenuptial agreement, he would have left after the first year. Now, he couldn't afford a divorce. He liked his lifestyle, but unfortunately the money was all hers. He couldn't live as he had for the last ten years on just his salary. She was so incredibly boring. She had enough money that they could have lived anywhere in the country, but she insisted on staying in Rosemount.

They still lived on the same street, in the same house, as when they were first married. She couldn't understand his need for the finer things in life. She was content to be the perfect little housewife. The only excitement in his life were the little affairs he had been having for most of their married life. She let him control her money. She had no idea just how much of it he had spent on other women.

He had seen Eleanor and was able to steer her away from the table before his wife had seen her. Eleanor had been furious. She demanded to know why he was seeing someone else. His good luck held, though, and she didn't seem to suspect that he was with his wife. Not that night. He thought he had convinced her to go home, but she had waited around in the parking lot until they left. The little snoop had taken the tag number from his wife's car and run it through the computer at work the next day at the Division of Motor Vehicles.

She was sitting in her car across the street from his house when he came home from work the next day. He had pretended not to see her, and she had driven away a few minutes later. He'd known then that there was going to be trouble, and he began making his plans. He called her at home the next afternoon. She had been cold on the phone, but agreed to meet him the following Saturday.

They had met at the mall in Charlotte. He had talked her into going for a drive with him. She was angry and demanded to know why he had deceived her. He told her that the marriage to his wife was one of convenience, and that she didn't love him any more than he loved her. He told her that his wife was the one who had all the affairs. He even managed to cry a little as he told her how he had wanted to have children, but that his wife was too concerned about losing her figure to get pregnant.

She had seemed to believe it all. He was sure that he was out of the woods until she said, "Maybe if I go to her and tell her how much we love each other, she'll give you a divorce. It won't be easy for me to marry a divorced man, but I love you so much, I know we can work this out."

The very thought of her talking to his wife had sent cold chills down his spine and made him feel like throwing up. He'd been able to fool his wife for ten years, and he wasn't going to let some naïve little fool mess it up now. He hid his anger and asked her to go for a drive with him to talk.

Eleanor continued to talk as they drove. She hadn't noticed his silence. He listened and his feelings of dread had grown to tantamount proportions. He'd known then that he had to do it. He'd come prepared. He couldn't let her ruin everything he had worked so hard for all these years.

She had been so busy planning their life together that she paid scant attention to where they were going. When he had turned onto the rutted dirt track that ran through the woods along county road CR 358, she had looked up in surprise. "What are we doing here?" she'd asked.

He'd turned to her and said, "I thought we might take a little moonlight stroll and make some plans for our future." She'd thrown her arms around his neck and cried tears of happiness.

What a little fool she'd been. She had clung to his arm as they walked deep into the woods away from the car. She'd prattled on and on incessantly. He hadn't listened, just nodded his head occasionally and that was all the response she'd needed.

When they were about a mile into the woods, he'd stopped and taken her into his arms. He'd kissed her passionately, and she'd responded just as she always had. He'd kissed and caressed her until she was breathless and seemed barely able to stand up. Eleanor told him that they had to stop. She couldn't do these things with him again until they were married.

Carefully, he slipped the knife from his waistband. She looked up into his eyes just as he stabbed her in the back. He watched her eyes widen, and then she started screaming and struggling to get away from him. He held her tightly and stabbed her several more times. She finally stopped screaming, and he let her fall to the ground

He watched her for a few minutes. Her eyes were wide open; her mouth frozen in a silent scream. Blood covered the simple white dress she'd worn and dripped onto the ground. Convinced that she was dead, he returned to the car to retrieve the shovel he'd brought along to bury her. Everything had gone just as planned, but when he returned with the shovel, Eleanor was gone.

In a state of panic, he looked for her, fear gnawing at his insides. He knew she couldn't have gotten far. She was too weak. The scarlet river on the ground was mute testament to just how badly she'd been injured. *She had to be close by,* he'd assured himself.

He shined the flashlight around the area, scanning the ground for any sign of her. He spotted marks in the leaves where she had dragged herself along. He'd followed the trail and found her lying near the tree line at the edge of CR 358. She wasn't moving, and her eyes were closed.

He leaned over to pick her up and take her farther back into the woods when he was caught in the glare of the headlights. Panicked, he looked up. Realizing his mistake, he started shouting for the driver to stop. He ran toward the car, not knowing what he was going to do.

The vehicle hesitated. Then, the engine raced, and the car left quickly. He couldn't see who was at the wheel, only that the car was a late model black Ford. He'd been scared then and raced back to his car and left. Only later had he realized that he dropped his flashlight and left the shovel near the spot where he had killed her.

He watched the paper for an account of the murder. On Monday, he read the newspaper story and was relieved that they had not yet released her name. Now he had more time to gather his thoughts and plan. He was sure that no one who knew him had seen them together.

He'd worn gloves that night so fingerprints wouldn't identify him. If only that car hadn't come along. Another ten minutes and he would have been deep into the woods with her body. He wondered how much the driver had seen.

The moon had been only a thin slice in the sky that night, and it had been very dark. He wished that he'd not yelled. Perhaps they hadn't heard. He'd wait now and watch.

The police would release information to the public through the paper. He'd bide his time and decide what his next move would be based on what he read and what he heard around town. Perhaps there was nothing to worry about.

The rain had certainly washed away much of the evidence. Since he didn't believe in God, he chalked it up to just another lucky break for him.

Five

It had been a long day for Connie. The children had been noisy and easily distracted. She'd tried all day not to think about Eleanor, but was unable to keep her thoughts from wandering. Several of the children had asked her what was wrong. "Why do you look so sad Miss Mitchell?" Thomas Morgan asked.

Thomas was one of her favorite students. He was a quiet boy with red hair and hazel eyes. He was well-liked by his peers. He was sensitive to the moods of others and always tried to cheer them up when they were sad. She had told him that she wasn't sad, just a little tired. She could see by the expression on his face that he didn't believe her.

For the remainder of the day, he tried in various ways to make her feel better. At the end of the day before he left, he gave her a hug and told her that tomorrow would be better.

Connie watched as he walked out of the room. *Things were so simple when you were eight or nine,* she thought. If only life stayed that simple when you were an adult. Shaking her head, she locked up the classroom and left.

She picked up a newspaper at the filling station where she stopped for gas. She wanted to wait until she was home to read the article about Eleanor.

Passing the crime scene, she noted that there were officers once more going over the area. She was surprised. She supposed that they were through with this part of the investigation. Driving slowly by, she saw Officer Cook among the team. He looked up and waved to her. She returned his greeting as she left.

She pulled into her drive and thought how beautiful the old place looked in the afternoon sun. Sunlight filtered through the leaves on the large maple just outside of her bedroom window. A few more weeks and the leaves will be gone, she thought. The weathermen were predicting an early winter this year.

The grass was still green and lush looking thanks to the wetter than normal conditions in late summer and early fall. The house was set near the front of a 25-acre piece of land.

Most of the property had not been cleared. She had someone come in a couple of times each year to clear the underbrush. She liked to be able to walk the woods without fear of tripping over the debris that fell from the trees.

She'd always loved walking in these woods, especially when her grandfather was alive. He had been a lover of nature and eagerly passed on his knowledge to his granddaughter. She missed him terribly and her grandmother as well. They had died within a few months of each other when she was only fifteen.

She paused now and listened as a light wind whispered through the stand of tall pines on the east side of the property. She loved the sound of the wind through the pines. It sounded differently than when it blew through the other trees on the place.

She walked toward the house and thought how much better it looked since she'd had it painted. The walls were a rich ivory; the trim a wonderful forest green.

The birds were once again at the feeder by the kitchen window. She enjoyed watching them. The cardinals and the doves were her favorites. She loved listening to the call of the mourning doves in the late afternoon.

Going up the steps, she unlocked the door and went inside. The house smelled somewhat musty, so she opened the windows in the living room and kitchen.

She changed into a pair of jeans and a pale blue sweater and went back to the kitchen. She peeled an orange and took it and the paper onto the front porch. Sitting in one of the rockers, she ate her snack and read the article about Eleanor's death.

She had been killed around ten Saturday night. The paper described in vivid detail the murder. Eleanor had been stabbed several times—all deep wounds—any of which could have killed her. She apparently survived long enough to drag herself to the edge of the woods where the body had been found. Following the trail through the woods, the police had come upon the site of the murder. They had found several items, including a shovel, near the site. The killer must have intended to bury his victim.

The paper speculated on what might have happened to stop him from completing the job. *Dear God,* Connie thought, *I'm the reason he didn't finish the job.* She continued reading. The police were still gathering evidence and expected to arrest a suspect soon. Connie assumed that they had found enough evidence at the scene to arrive at a suspect. She knew she had been of little help with her meager description of the man she had seen.

The article gave the time and place of the funeral and listed members of Eleanor's family who had come into town for the service.

Just then, Connie heard the phone ringing. Jumping up, she hurried inside to answer it. It was Erin. Connie could tell from her voice that she had been crying.

"Oh Connie," she cried. "Have you heard the news about Eleanor?"

"I was just reading the story in the paper," she told her.

"I can't believe that something so horrible happened to her," Erin said. "She was so sweet. Who could have done such a terrible thing to her?"

"I don't know why anyone would have wanted to hurt Eleanor," Connie replied. "Whoever it was, he must be a monster."

"Do you think it was someone she knew," Erin asked. "I've always heard that most murders are committed by someone the victim knows."

Connie remembered Greg having made that same comment to her. She was quiet as she thought about some of the men Eleanor had dated. There had been many over the last year. Most of them had seemed harmless enough. A few had been looking for someone to support them. Of the ones she had met, Connie couldn't remember any particular one that had seemed like the type to do something this evil. But Connie knew she had not met all of the men that Eleanor had dated.

These were the ones Eleanor had met at the club in Charlotte. Connie had warned her about the kind of men that she might meet there. Eleanor had laughed and called Connie an old mother hen. She told her that she was always careful and made sure to meet them in crowded places for their dates.

Connie remembered that for the last couple of months, Eleanor had been very happy. She had told Connie that she had finally met the man she wanted to marry. She was somewhat reticent when Connie had questioned her about him, though. At the time, Connie had shrugged it off and assumed Eleanor wanted to keep the details to herself until she became engaged. Now she wondered. Maybe she had better tell Greg about that.

The sound of Erin's voice brought her abruptly back to the present. "Hey, are you still there?" Erin asked. "I thought we'd gotten cut off. I know how these phone lines are when it's windy."

"I was just thinking about Eleanor," she replied. "I can't believe that she's dead."

"The paper says the funeral will be on Saturday," Erin said. "Do you think the choir will be asked to sing?"

"I guess it depends on what the family wants," she replied. "I'm sure most of us will be there regardless."

Erin was quiet for a minute and then said, "I suppose Russ will call everyone once he knows. We will need to practice. It's been quite a while since we last sang for a funeral and I know he'll want something really special for Eleanor. I'm sure everyone will be as shocked as we were when they read the paper."

Again, Connie was silent. She couldn't tell Erin that her own shock had come days ago, on her way to church. Since that time, she had been somewhat numb. The only time the numbness seemed to lift was when she was with Greg. She realized she had been quiet for too long and said, "Yes, I'm sure that they will be."

They talked for a few minutes longer and then said good-bye. The sun was setting, and Connie decided to stay inside. It was about the time she usually ate dinner, but she didn't feel in the least hungry. She decided to do some laundry and tidy up the house a bit. It was mindless work, and Connie's thoughts wandered back to the murder. She remembered the last time she had seen Eleanor.

She had been radiant with happiness and eagerly looking forward to making wedding plans. Connie had listened to her and been happy for her. She had not asked for details because Eleanor didn't seemed to want to share too much information.

"You're going to love him," she had told Connie. "He is handsome, charming, funny, and rich."

Jokingly, Connie had asked, "Do you think he has a twin brother?"

Eleanor had gotten a strange look on her face and then said. "I really don't know much about his family. He says he doesn't want to share our happiness with anyone else yet. He wouldn't be pleased that I've told you this much."

Connie had been troubled by her remark and wanted to ask more questions, but someone else had walked up and Eleanor had gotten quiet. Later, Connie had looked for her, but she had already gone.

Connie had shrugged off her troubling doubts and gone home. She wished now she'd called and tried to talk to Eleanor later. She wondered if she should call Greg and tell him some of what she had just remembered. Just thinking about talking to him lifted her gloomy spirits. She decided that she would go by the police station after school tomorrow and see him in person.

She finished her laundry, had a cup of tea, and read until bedtime. She knelt beside her bed and offered the Rosary she prayed for Eleanor's soul. When she was finished, she brushed her teeth, took a quick shower, and went to bed.

She dreamed about Eleanor and her mysterious man. Eleanor was weeping, and the man whose face Connie could never see was berating her angrily. He then turned his back to her and left. Eleanor was begging now, and Connie could see the look of anguish in her eyes.

The man turned back to her and lifted his arm high into the air. Eleanor's look changed to one of panic, and she began to run.

Now Connie was Eleanor, and her pursuer chased her relentlessly through her dreams for the rest of the night. She looked back and tried to see his face, but to no avail. She could hear his voice, though; a terrifying sound that filled her heart with dread.

Once again, she awakened in a cold sweat with tears on her face. She didn't want to remember the dream, but couldn't seem to forget. If only she could remember the face of the man she had seen.

Six

Connie gave up trying to go back to sleep and sat in her kitchen, watching as the sun rose. She showered, dressed, and left for work at seven. She was tired, and the day loomed long before her. Still, she loved her work and just being with the children made her feel better. The thought of seeing Greg that afternoon didn't hurt either.

After lunch, she did some listening exercises with the kids. As usual, they threw themselves wholeheartedly into this lesson. Connie found herself listening more closely than usual, straining to remember what it was about the voice she'd heard. It was a futile effort, though, and she was glad when the dismissal bell rang.

She pulled into the parking lot at the police station around 3:45. She saw that Greg's Mustang was parked in the lot. She didn't know the number of the squad car he drove, so she could only hope that he was here. Going in, she inquired about him at the reception area. She was told that he was on his way back in and she could wait if she wished to speak to him.

Connie went back outside to wait for him. It was a beautiful fall day, and she hated being cooped up inside when the weather was so nice. She sat on a bench, under a large spreading oak tree. A light breeze wafted through her hair and brought the scent of freshly mown grass with it. She breathed deeply and relaxed. She closed her eyes and waited peacefully. She must have drifted off to sleep because a slight pressure on her shoulder startled her.

Greg had been thinking about Connie a lot today. He wanted to get to know her better and had decided to call her when he got back to the station. Pulling into the parking lot, he was surprised to see her sitting on the bench. He parked the car and walked over to her.

As he came closer, he could see that her eyes were closed. *She looks so peaceful sitting there,* he thought. He loved the way her beautiful auburn hair ruffled as the breeze moved through it. It came just below her chin and turned under slightly all around. It looked healthy and was full of beautiful highlights.

Her mouth looked soft and made him want to kiss her. She didn't seem to wear a lot of makeup, and he liked that. He hated the way women looked when they wore too much makeup, like painted dolls. Connie was sweet and, to his eyes, naturally beautiful.

She didn't open her eyes, and he stood and stared down at her for a couple of minutes. *She must be tired,* he thought. He knew she hadn't been sleeping well since the murder. He wished he could help her more. He really cared for her and was surprised by the depths of his feelings. He normally didn't get involved this quickly. He'd been hurt a few years before and had guarded his emotions carefully since then. Connie had gotten past that barrier and right into his heart. He laid his hand gently on her shoulder. She jumped, and her eyes flew open.

Connie looked up at Greg and smiled sweetly. He sat on the bench beside her, and they chatted about their day for a minute. Then he asked, "Are you here to see me? Is everything okay?"

"I remembered some things about Eleanor last night, and I thought they might be helpful in your investigation," she said. "Do you have time to talk now?".

Greg said quietly, "I always have time for you, Connie, even if it's not about the case."

Connie thought that was the sweetest thing any guy had ever said to her. She looked at Greg and smiled tremulously.

"Why don't we go into my office and I'll take your statement. After we're done, maybe you'd like to have dinner with me?" Greg stood and, taking Connie's arm, walked beside her into the station and into his office. When they were seated, he picked Eleanor's file up and opened it. "Now tell me what you've remembered," he told her.

Connie told him of her last conversation with Eleanor and how she had been so reticent about the man she was dating. She also told him about the club in Charlotte that Eleanor had frequented. He made notes as she was talking, and when she was finished he said, "This could be very helpful. We don't have many leads right now and this is something new we can check. Most of the men she dated have already come forth and been cleared. They all denied having been with her for the last couple of months, though. We can't seem to find anyone who knows the identity of the last man she dated. Maybe someone at this club will recall who she was seen with recently."

Connie nodded and said, "I wish I'd tried to get more information from her, but she was so evasive when I talked to her, and I didn't want to pry. If only I had been more persistent."

"People in love do funny things," Greg said. "I'm sure there is nothing more you could have done or said that would have made any difference."

"You're probably right," Connie said. "Still, I can't help feeling guilty for not having tried to get more information from her. Maybe I could have saved her life."

"You've got to stop beating yourself up over this, Connie. Eleanor was a grown woman, and she knew what she was doing," Greg replied forcefully. He hated to see her so upset.

"Why don't we go and get some dinner now? I know a great little Italian place just up the street. The guys and I have lunch there sometime. The food is fantastic."

Mario's was a small restaurant on the ground floor of an old office building. A group of attorneys occupied the top two floors of the historic brick edifice.

The décor was typical of most small Italian places. The lighting was dim, and the music played softly in the background. Small tables sat in the shadows around a small dance floor. They both ordered a glass of Chianti and the chicken parmigiana. They talked quietly over dinner and had coffee and tiramisu afterwards.

Other couples danced around the small floor, and Greg asked if she would like to dance. Connie had been hoping he would ask. She wanted to feel his strong arms around her again. She remembered how safe she had felt in them before. She nodded, and taking her arm, he led her to the floor.

They danced, enjoying being in each other's arms. Greg couldn't remember when he had felt so complete with a woman. She was something special. He tightened his hold on her, and she nestled closer to him.

They were the last couple to leave the floor, and Greg's arms felt strangely empty without Connie in them. She, too, seemed reluctant to have the moment end.

He drove her back to the station to pick up her car and followed her home. It was not quite nine o'clock, and Connie invited him in for a cup of coffee. He accepted eagerly, and they spent the remainder of the evening sharing their coffee and sitting on her front porch. He stood up reluctantly around 10:30 to leave.

Connie stood also. "Thank you for a lovely dinner," she said. "I had a wonderful time. I was feeling pretty low earlier, but I feel much better now."

Greg smiled, "I'm glad I could help. I had a great time, too. I hope we can do this again."

"Next time, we'll eat here," Connie said.

Greg hesitated and then said, "Connie, I'm going to kiss you goodnight." Reaching out, he pulled her into his arms. She melted against him, and he kissed her firmly on the lips. She responded so sweetly that he was reluctant to end the embrace.

When he finally ended the kiss, they were both breathless. Connie stepped back from his embrace and ran her shaking fingers through her hair. She'd been kissed many times before, but couldn't remember ever feeling this way after. She felt lightheaded, as if she had just run a marathon. She noticed that Greg, too, seemed to be having trouble with his own breathing. She hoped he was feeling the same way she was.

Greg breathed deeply of the cool night air. He hadn't expected to be so deeply affected by just a kiss. He wanted to kiss her again, but managed to restrain the impulse. They had known each other for such a short time, and he didn't want to rush her. When he was able to think coherently, he said, "I want to see you again, soon. Would you like to have dinner on Friday?"

Connie was going to say yes when she remembered Eleanor's funeral on Saturday. "I'd like that very much, but Eleanor's viewing will probably be that night and I want to be there. Also, if we are going to be singing, the choir will probably practice after that. Perhaps we'd better not make any plans before Sunday. I'll be free after about noon."

Greg didn't want to wait until Sunday to see her again, but knew he had little choice but to agree. He wanted to give her time to mourn her friend, but he also wanted to be available if she needed him.

"Sunday afternoon will be fine," he said. "If you should need me before then, though, please call. Let me give you my home number in case you can't reach me at the office." He pulled one of his father's business cards from his wallet and wrote his number on it. He handed it to Connie and started down the steps to his car. He stopped when she called softly to him.

"Wait," she said. Coming down the steps, she reached up and kissed him on the cheek. "I just wanted you to know how very special tonight was for me. If I get a chance, I'll call you on Saturday."

He waited until she was safely inside before he left. He found himself singing all the way home. His last thought before he went to sleep was that Saturday couldn't get here fast enough.

Connie watched through the window as he drove down the road. There was a message on her machine from Russell, the choir director. They would be singing for the funeral, and he wanted to practice after the viewing on Friday. He wanted Connie to sing a solo. She hoped she would be able to get through the song without breaking down. Even the thought of Eleanor's funeral was not enough to dim her happiness completely.

She smiled to herself as she got ready for bed. When she said her prayers, she offered a special one to God for bringing Greg into her life. Her only regret was that it had not been under happier circumstances. No faceless strangers inhabited her dreams tonight. She dreamed of Greg's kiss and his warm embrace.

Seven

She was up before the alarm went off the next morning and was still feeling euphoric. She knew that it would be a difficult day and her thoughts of Greg would help her to deal with everything. The day at work passed quickly and she was home by 4 p.m. She ate a light supper and read for a short time.

Around 5:30, she dressed for the viewing. She wore a navy blue chemise and navy pumps. She left for the funeral home at 6:15. The viewing was to begin at seven, and she wanted to be there a little early.

The parking lot was nearly full by the time Connie arrived. She was greeted at the door by an usher and asked to sign the guest book. Erin came through the door just as she was finishing. They hugged and took seats near the back of the small chapel.

They prayed silently until Father Murphy entered and began the Rosary. When it was done, they filed up to take a last look at their friend. Tears were streaming down their faces as they looked down at Eleanor. Being here reminded Connie of her parents' funeral, and she could barely control her sobbing. Erin took her by the arm and led her out to the lobby.

Soon, she was able to regain her composure. They both returned to the chapel. Eleanor's father was going to speak to the mourners.

He was a tall, distinguished man, with silver hair and sad gray eyes. His eulogy for his daughter was beautiful. He told of her zest for life, her trusting nature, and her kindness. His eyes glistened with tears as he told them how much she had loved her life in Rosemount and how she had enjoyed the many friends she had made there.

When he was done, he leaned over the casket, kissed his daughter one last time, and returned to his seat. Eleanor's mother was sobbing uncontrollably as he led her away from the casket.

Connie had hoped to speak with them, but she could see that now was not the time.

She and Erin stayed for another half-hour, praying and visiting with other friends. At 8:30, they left for the church to practice.

Russell handed the group a list of songs that Eleanor's parents had requested, and they went over these. Connie solo was to be "Amazing Grace." She went through it three times with the organist and then left for home.

Connie lay in bed and listened to the old house creak and groan as it always did. She was having a difficult time getting to sleep. She was very tired, but her mind was filled with thoughts of Eleanor. She kept seeing her face as she lay in the coffin. It hadn't looked much like her. She supposed it never really did. Connie finally cried herself to sleep.

The rain drumming on the roof awakened Connie around 8 a.m. It was dark and dreary- looking outside. *A fitting day for a funeral*, she thought.

After her shower, she had some breakfast at the kitchen table. There were no birds at the feeder this morning. She washed her few dishes and returned to her room to dress. The black dress she put on was the same one she had worn for her parents' funeral. It was a simple dress with no adornment. She slipped into a pair of black pumps and pinned a black-and-tan-printed scarf to the neck of the dress. The onyx earrings and ring she wore had belonged to her mother.

She brushed her hair and applied her makeup. Glancing into the mirror, she noticed that she was looking a little paler than normal. *Probably the result of too little sleep*, she thought.

The phone rang around ten. It was Keith Thomas, the carpenter. He wanted to know if she was going to be home later that afternoon. He had some free time and wanted to come by and fix her door. Connie told him she would not be available until Monday. She didn't like to make others work on Sunday. He assured her that Monday would be fine. He planned to come by around 4 p.m.

She had scarcely replaced the receiver when the phone rang once more. This time Erin was on the other end. She wanted to ride into town with Connie. Her car was once again acting up. It was a fickle piece of machinery, which ran only when it wanted to.

The funeral Mass was to begin at noon. It would be followed by a reception in the parish hall. Connie and Erin both belonged to the parish outreach committee that was hosting the reception. They needed to arrive early to help set up.

Connie hurried through the driving rain, wishing once again for that garage. She went about three miles north on CR 358 and then turned onto a small clay road. The road was slippery from the rain, and she drove carefully.

Erin lived in a small guesthouse on her parents' property. She'd always been close to them and was happy with the arrangement. Her parents liked having her close as well. Connie pulled up as close to the door as she could and honked the horn loudly. Erin came out and dashed to the car. Slipping into the passenger seat, she shook the water from her hair. Connie noticed that Erin, too, looked pale.

"What a dreary day," she said. "This weather is a perfect match for the way I feel."

Connie nodded in agreement and put the car in gear. They talked quietly on the way into town. Erin asked Connie to stop at the bakery to pick up a cake she had ordered for the reception. Connie waited in the car while Erin ran into the store. She returned in a few minutes with the cake. She held it on her lap as they drove to the church.

The parish hall was a small wood frame building to the right of the church. It was almost as old as the church itself. It had served as a meeting place for the parish for nearly a hundred years. The members of the church kept it in good repair. The oak plank floors had been refinished just that summer. The walls were oak as well.

The place was busy as people hurried about setting up tables and chairs. The nonperishable food was set on the tables along the wall. Mourners would help themselves to food and drink. Outreach members would keep the trays and coffeepot filled. She and Erin helped until everything was set up.

They walked with other church members under the covered walkway that connected the hall and church. The small pews in the small church were already filled. Anyone coming later would have to stand. Connie was not surprised. Eleanor had been a favorite with church members. Many would feel the loss of her friendship.

She noticed that there were a number of people she did not recognize as being part of the parish. These must be people Eleanor had worked with and known in the community. She recognized several of the men Eleanor had dated in the past. She wondered if her most recent male friend was present.

She and Erin took their places in the choir loft. The organist was playing softly. She studied her music and watched as more mourners crowded into the church. There were people standing everywhere.

The bell rang, and Father Murphy came onto the altar followed by the acolytes. The smell of incense drifted through the air. Everyone stood, and the choir began to sing. Eleanor's parents had chosen very traditional music and the sounds of "How Great Thou Art" filled the small church. The incense swirled around the casket that had been placed in the center aisle. All through the Mass Connie could hear weeping. She, too, was very close to tears.

Her solo would be after Communion, and she prayed she would not break down. She didn't. She put everything she had into her song and offered it to God for Eleanor. When she was done, the church was silent. The closing hymn, "Just a Closer Walk with Thee," reverberated through the building. There was silence then, as the casket was wheeled down the aisle and into the hearse. Eleanor was to be buried in the family plot in Ashville.

The reception lasted for about two hours. Connie was able to speak for a few minutes to Eleanor's parents. They were thankful that she'd had such good friends in town and appreciated all the effort that had gone into the Mass and reception. They hugged Connie and told her how much Eleanor would have enjoyed her song.

By 4:30, the cleanup of the hall was completed. Connie and Erin stayed and talked with other members of the group until around five. The rain was still coming down in torrents when they went outside. Connie drove slowly through the downpour. The windshield wipers worked furiously to keep the glass clear. Still, it was hard to see. The temperature had already dropped below fifty degrees, and it was getting colder by the minute.

Connie turned the heat on, and she and Erin were silent until she turned of the highway onto CR 358.

"Would you like to stay the night with me?" Erin asked. "I could sure use the company. Mom and Dad are out of town 'til tomorrow, and it's been kind of lonely."

Connie thought for a moment and then nodded. "I'll drop you off and then go home to pick up a few things. I'll be over in about an hour. I have some calls I need to make."

She dropped Erin off and drove home. Parking as close to the house as she could, she dashed to the porch. The front door had swelled again and was hard to close. *Thank goodness Keith is coming Monday,* she thought as she struggled to close it.

She changed into a pair of jeans, a bulky cotton sweater, and some boots. She sat at the table in the kitchen and called the number Greg had written on the card. She assumed that since it was so late he would be at home, not at the office. She let it ring about six times and then hung up, disappointed.

She packed her things and left for Erin's. The rain was still coming down in buckets. She didn't hear the phone ringing as she locked the door behind her.

Greg saw the indicator light flashing on his caller ID when he came into his bedroom after his shower. There was no message on his machine, and the number was unavailable on the caller ID screen. He wondered if it had been Connie. He had memorized her number from the initial check he had run. Picking up the phone, he dialed her number. He let it ring for a minute or so and then hung up. He guessed he'd have to wait until tomorrow to talk to her. He noticed that it was still raining and had gotten colder. He decided to stay in, so he fixed himself a frozen dinner.

While he was eating, he read over the Lincoln file again. The dead woman had been well-liked in the community. She had not lived in the area very long, but was very active.

She worked at the DMV full time, was active in her church, sang in the choir, volunteered at the local blood bank, and had a busy social life as well. He wondered when she'd had time to sleep.

The men she'd dated over the last few months had been ruled out as suspects. He reviewed the latest information Connie had given him and decided to check out the club in Charlotte Eleanor had frequented. Perhaps someone there would remember the last man she had been with at the club. He closed the file around midnight and went to bed.

Connie and Erin sat and talked about Eleanor and the good times they'd had together. Around nine, they fixed a pot of tea, some scrambled eggs and toast. They cleaned up the dishes and by eleven o'clock, they were both ready for bed. The rain was still coming down. Connie hoped that it would be gone by morning. She said her Rosary and went to bed.

Eight

Erin stuck her head in the door around 7:30 a.m. and saw that Connie was still sleeping. She walked to the bed and shook her gently. "Hey," she said. "It's time to get up. We don't want to be late for Mass."

Connie couldn't believe how soundly she'd slept. She didn't remember dreaming at all.

They showered, dressed, and left for Mass at 8:15. The rain had stopped, and a cold front had come through during the night.

The morning sun was bright, and the sky was a beautiful azure blue. Water droplets glistened on the grass and the fallen leaves. A light breeze moved through the trees, and droplets fell as they walked to the car. They didn't have time to try Erin's car, so Connie drove once more.

The church was filled to capacity this morning. There was talk of building a larger church, but no details had been settled. The choir always sang at this Mass, and Eleanor's spot was conspicuously empty. *She'll be missed by everyone*, Connie thought. After Mass, they returned to Erin's house. She invited Connie in for breakfast.

"I appreciate the offer," she said, "but I really need to get home. I need to work on my lesson plans for the week." She hugged Erin and waited till she had gone inside, then drove home.

The light on the answering machine was flashing when Connie got home. She was hoping the message would be from Greg. It wasn't. Keith Thomas had called to let her know that he would be unable to come by on Monday. His wife had been in an accident and she had broken her leg. Her mother would be coming on Wednesday to take care of their children, but until then he was needed at home. He recommended another carpenter if she was in a hurry to get the job done. *A few more days wouldn't make any difference*, she thought. The weather was getting colder by the day. Rainfall would probably be minimal for the next few months. She could probably put it off till spring if need be. His was the only message.

She changed her clothes, had a bite to eat, and settled in her office to work on lesson plans. She became engrossed in the work and lost track of time. Hunger forced her to go to the kitchen. She was amazed to see that it was already 3 p.m. She remembered her promise to call Greg and picked up the phone. She dialed his home number. He answered after the second ring.

Greg had awakened early that morning. He'd gone to church in Blue Springs with his family. They all belonged to St. Bridget's parish there. He enjoyed being with his family, but when they asked him to come home for dinner, he declined. He wanted to be home if Connie called. His mother laughed and said, "She must be something special for you to turn down Sunday dinner." He'd just kissed her and said nothing.

He'd gone home and spent the day straightening up the place. He was finishing the kitchen when the phone rang. It was Connie.

"I'm sorry it's so late in the day," she said. "I was doing my lesson plans and lost track of time."

"No problem," he replied. "I was just doing some chores that I'd been putting off all week. How did everything go yesterday?"

"It was a beautiful service," she said. "Even the rain couldn't change that. I called last night, but you didn't answer."

"That must have been when I was in the shower. Your number wasn't listed on the caller ID, but I thought it might have been you. I called back, but no one answered."

"My machine should have picked up," Connie said. "What time did you call?"

"Shortly after seven," he answered.

"That was about the same time Mr. Thomas called. He must have been leaving his message when you were trying to get through."

"It's a beautiful afternoon. Would you like to go for a drive?" Greg asked.

"That would be nice," she said. "Pick me up in about half an hour."

Greg agreed, and they rang off the phone. Connie changed into a nicer pair of jeans and a periwinkle blue sweater. She washed her face and cleaned her teeth. She brushed her hair till it shone and applied fresh makeup.

She had just finished when she heard the knock at the door and hurried to open it. He was leaning against the porch rail. He looked so handsome in his jeans and navy sweater. She was glad she had spent extra time getting ready. He smiled at her, and his strong white teeth gleamed.

She looks fantastic, he thought. Not as pale as she had been the last few days. He hoped he had been the one to bring the rosy hue to her cheeks. In the past, he had been attracted to a different type of woman. He'd liked them tall, slim, and witty—women who made no demands on his time. His relationships had been short. He loved his work and wasn't willing to cut back on the time he spent at the station.

In just a week, Connie had changed all that. He found himself wanting to spend more time with her and less time with his case files. He was thirty-five and thought he'd finally found a woman he could spend the rest of his life with, easily.

Connie stepped onto the porch and pulled the door shut behind her. It was swollen again from the damp and didn't want to close easily.

Greg noticed the trouble she was having with the door. "Here, let me try," he said.

Gratefully, she stepped aside. He pulled firmly and was then able to close the door.

"Do you have that problem often?" he asked.

"Only when it's been raining a lot," she said. "The carpenter was supposed to come tomorrow, but he called and canceled. He had a family emergency."

"If he doesn't get to it soon, let me know. Maybe I could look at it for you," he said.

Greg opened the car door for her, and she slid in the seat. He took his place behind the wheel and started the engine. "I think we'll have the top up today," he said. "The temperature is supposed to drop into the forties before sunset."

"They're predicting an early first freeze. Maybe as soon as next week," Connie said.

They drove in silence for a time, enjoying the scenery and their time together. The silence was comfortable, as if they were two friends who had known each other forever.

Connie glanced at his hands on the wheel. They were large, capable hands, tanned a dark brown, with nails that were blunt cut and clean.

He turned his head and smiled. They had been driving for about an hour now. It was getting dark and cold. Greg turned the heat up and asked if she'd like to stop somewhere for dinner. They were coming into Asheville, and there were plenty of places to choose from. He asked her if she had any preferences.

"I like all kinds of food," she said. "You choose."

"How about Cracker Barrel then? They have something to please just about any taste. I love their breakfasts myself."

Connie grinned. She couldn't believe how much alike they were. Whenever she was on a road trip, she loved to eat at Cracker Barrel. It was her favorite place to stop. She loved the food and the shopping.

It was dinnertime, and the place was packed. They had to wait forty minutes for a table.

She and Greg looked around the store for a while, then sat out on the porch in the cold night air. They shared a double rocker, and she was grateful for his closeness. They talked about his job, and she asked, "What do you do with your off time?"

"Until lately, I worked," he said bluntly, looking at her intently.

Connie felt her face warming, and she looked down at her hands. Greg reached over and touched her hand. He started to speak just as the hostess called them to their table. "We'll talk later," he said.

Seated at the table, they both ordered from the breakfast menu. She ordered French toast, sausage, and coffee. Greg ordered pork chops, eggs, potatoes, toast, and coffee. They talked of everyday affairs as they ate, neither wanting to talk about the case tonight.

Later, on the long drive home they listened to classical music on the CD player Greg had installed in the car. Connie found herself thinking about all the events of the past week.

She felt as if she had been on a roller coaster ride, up one minute and down the next.

Dealing with Eleanor's death had been difficult. It had awakened emotions she hadn't dealt with since the death of her parents. She had latched onto Greg like a child to a security blanket. She liked him so much, but she knew she needed time to deal with the events of the past week on her own. When she had done that, she would be able to honestly examine her feelings for him and go from there. She was sure of only one thing: She didn't want to hurt him.

He pulled into her drive and cut the engine. Turning to her he said, "We need to talk about some things, Connie. I know it's not pleasant for you to discuss the case, but I really need to talk something over with you. I'd also like to talk about us."

"I guess we do at that." she said. "Things seem to be moving very fast. We've known each other barely a week, and I think we need to slow down a bit."

This wasn't what Greg wanted to hear, but for now he was willing to capitulate. "If that's what you want, I'm willing to go along for now. I know this has been sudden, but I've never been surer of anything than I am right now. I want you to be just as sure. I can wait."

He continued, "Now about the case. I'm planning to visit the club where Eleanor was seen several times in the last few months. If I get a lead on our mystery man, I'd like for you to come in and look at some more pictures."

"I can do that," she said. "I want to help you catch the monster that did this to her."

Greg nodded approvingly. "I was sure you'd feel that way. I'll call when I have something for you. Now let's get you inside, out of the cold." He took her arm and walked her to the door. He waited patiently while she unlocked it, then pushed it open for her. He wanted to kiss her again, but decided against it. He'd promised her time, and he wasn't going back on his word.

Connie thanked him for a lovely evening and watched as he left. Closing the door, she felt emptiness inside and wondered if she'd been too hasty. She wanted to feel his arms around her again and the warmth of his lips on hers. Watching from the window, she saw him lift his hand in farewell as he pulled out of the driveway. She prepared for bed, but once more had difficulty getting to sleep. She read from her Bible for a while, then turned out the light. When sleep finally came, so did the dream. That same voice called to her all through the night, and she awakened more tired than when she'd gone to bed.

Nine

Her day at school was difficult. She was short on patience and found herself being overly sharp with the children. When she chastised Thomas for taking too long to do his math, his face fell. She felt awful and apologized. He smiled and said, "That's okay, Miss Mitchell." She knew it wasn't, though. This whole ordeal was wearing her down. She'd never snapped at the kids this way before. She was going to have to find her way back to normal.

Connie played the listening game with the kids after lunch. It was her way of making up to them for her short temper. They were quick to forgive, as young children are, and by the end of the day everything was back on an even keel, at least at school.

Driving home, she found herself hoping that Greg might call. She wondered how much time he was going to give her. She wasn't even sure anymore that she wanted time. In just a week, he had become an important part of her life. Maybe she'd been wrong to suggest the time apart. She'd wait a couple of days and see how she felt then. If it were anything like she was feeling now, she'd probably be the one calling him.

Erin called around 5:30 and asked for a ride to choir practice. She had been unable to get her car started again. Connie picked her up. Later, on the drive home, Erin mentioned that she'd tried to call the previous evening. "I thought you were staying home," she said. "I wanted to let you know that Mom and Dad were staying over in Florida a few more days. You know how I hate staying alone without them close by. I was hoping you'd invite me to be your houseguest until they get back. Also, I still can't get the beast started and wanted to borrow your truck."

Connie laughed. She did indeed know how Erin felt about staying alone. She had felt the same way after her parents had died. It had taken her many months to get used to being alone at night. She still didn't like it, but she was able to cope. It had been a lot easier until the dreams started. Having Erin around for a couple of days would be a godsend. "That would be great," she answered. "We can laze around at night reading, playing cards, and watching TV. And you can cook." Erin was a great cook.

"I was pretty sure you'd say yes. I've already packed my bags," Erin said with a cocky grin. "If you don't mind waiting a few minutes, I'll run in and get them."

She was back in less than five minutes. "I had to check the messages and put the phone on call forwarding. You never know when Mr. Right is going to call. I wouldn't want to miss that. By the way, how is Lieutenant Reed these days?" she asked with a sly grin.

Connie wasn't quite sure how to answer that. She knew Erin would think she was nuts for pushing Greg away and maybe she was. She was already missing him, and it had been less than twenty-four hours. "He's fine," she said quietly. "We're going to take things a little slower, though."

Erin looked at Connie as though she'd grown two heads. "Are you out of your mind? A guy like that doesn't just drop into your lap every day of the week. I've done some checking on him, and he's almost perfect. He's never been married, doesn't smoke, drink or curse excessively, he's got a reputation for being a gentleman, and best of all, he's Catholic."

Now Connie was the one who was astounded. She hadn't known he was Catholic. They had never gotten around to talking about religion. "How did you find out all of that?"

Erin laughed. "I have my ways. But seriously, what's going on? I know you've had a rough week, but he seems to have been the one bright spot in all the ugliness."

"You're right," Connie said. "That's part of the problem. I need to know if what I'm feeling is real. Am I still going to feel the same way a few months from now when things are back to normal? Maybe I'm just leaning on him because he's a nice guy and I needed someone for support. I have to find out. The only way I can do that is to distance myself from him and deal with these emotions on my own."

Erin shook her head. "You may be right, but I still think you're crazy," she said affectionately.

"You're probably right, but I have to know for sure. I hope he's willing to wait," Connie replied as she pulled into her drive.

There were no messages on her machine. She didn't know if she was relieved or disappointed, perhaps a little of both. She and Erin talked for a short time and then went to bed.

Greg was sure Connie had no idea how difficult it had been for him not to call. He'd wanted to hear her voice even if it was on her machine. He'd worked late and tried not to think about her. Work, which had filled his life before, was no longer sufficient. Disgusted with himself, he'd finally gone home around 10 p.m. Maybe tomorrow would be better. Maybe she'd call him. *Right*, he thought. He knew she wouldn't. He'd seen the determination in her eyes. She was going to take all the time she needed. He just hoped it wouldn't be too long. Lying in bed, he pictured her as she'd been at dinner last night; her amber eyes glowing with laughter, her full lips curved in a smile. He drifted off to sleep with the image of her smiling face implanted firmly in his mind.

As Connie and Erin sat at the breakfast table the following morning, Connie remembered what Erin had said about Greg. "By the way," she asked, "how did you get so much information on Greg?"

Erin looked up from the plate of eggs she was consuming and said, "I asked Dad. You know he's friends with Sheriff Fowler. Adam Fowler couldn't say enough good things about the man. He said he expects Lieutenant Reed to be sheriff himself one day."

The remainder of the week passed quickly. She and Erin had a great time, as they always did when they were together. On Friday, Erin returned home. Connie was once again alone. She spent the weekend catching up on chores and working outside. She turned down several invitations from friends. She needed the time alone. She had a great deal of thinking to do. There was nothing like mindless labor to allow one to do just that.

From Greg, she heard nothing. The weather had turned colder, and the first freeze came Sunday night.

Greg spent the week working on the Lincoln case. He reread the autopsy report and studied the information that had come in since the woman's death. Her car had been found at a shopping mall the day after her body was discovered. Unable to locate the owner, mall security had the car towed. The towing company tried to locate the owner, with no success. On Wednesday, they had notified the Charlotte Police, who in turn had notified the Rosemount police after tracing the tag. The car was impounded and towed to the police lot in Rosemount.

The forensics team had taken four sets of prints from the car. They all had been identified, and none of the owners of the prints proved to be a viable suspect.

Greg visited the club in Charlotte and showed the victim's picture around. The bartender, who worked on weekends, recognized her, but had been unable to remember anyone in particular she had spent time with at the club. *Another dead end*, he thought.

The description given by Connie had proved to be of little help. With no distinguishing characteristics, the description fit any number of men who frequented the club. Hell, it even fit him.

Disgusted, he'd returned to the office and read the file once again. The victim had lived in a small house on the outskirts of town. He had talked to her neighbors and friends. They all had been appalled by the murder and no one was able to identify her latest male friend.

The house had been dusted for prints, with no luck. The house was immaculate. Eleanor had apparently been very neat. The only prints lifted belonged to the victim. Greg went over the crime scene again with the forensics team. Nothing new had been found.

The shovel and flashlight they had originally found could be bought at any local hardware store. No prints had been obtained from those either. By the end of the week, he was tired and frustrated. He missed being able to talk to Connie. He realized how empty his life had been before he met her.

On Friday night, he went out with some of the guys from the station. He had a good time, but knew it wasn't what he wanted to do every Friday night.

He spent Saturday with his brother James, helping put up a fence. He had dinner with James and his family and fell into bed exhausted around midnight.

After church on Sunday, he had dinner with his folks. His mom asked him when he was going to bring his new love for a visit. He answered tersely, "Mom, give it a rest." She had taken note of his tightlipped answer and changed the subject. He left soon after. He hadn't wanted to hurt his mother but he didn't want to talk about Connie either. He called before he went to bed and apologized.

Monday dawned cold and clear. There was frost on the ground, and Connie shivered as she walked to the car. She noticed that the leaves were gone from all but the evergreens now and realized that Thanksgiving was in just ten days.

She had spent last Thanksgiving with Erin and her family, so she was sure they would invite her again.

She wondered if there had been any new developments in Eleanor's case. The story was no longer front-page news. In fact, the paper hadn't mentioned anything about the case at all. She supposed that must mean there was nothing new. Maybe she would call Greg.

She shook her head. He'd said he would keep her informed, and she was sure he would be true to his word.

The day passed rapidly, and Connie decided to stop at the market before she went home. On her way out of the store, she bumped into a tall, dark-haired man who was leaning against the newsstand. He was silent as she apologized. However, she didn't care for the look in his eyes as he ran them over her body. She felt her face growing warm and quickly walked away from him. She could feel his eyes staring after her. That kind of scrutiny always made her uncomfortable. She managed to brush off her distaste and enjoy the drive home.

Ten

He'd seen nothing new in the paper this last week. The little fool was buried and hopefully his secret with her. On his way home, he'd gotten rid of the purse she'd left in the car. He'd gotten home around midnight that night, but managed to convince his wife that he'd been home by ten.

She always fell asleep in front of the TV when she waited up for him and that night had been no exception. He'd slipped in the back door and up the stairs to their room, where he showered and changed. He'd rumpled the bed to look as if he'd been in it, and then gone downstairs to wake her up. "You should have woke me up when you got home," she said. "I fell asleep around nine. I was trying to wait up."

He'd smiled that smile of his and carried her upstairs. He'd made love to her, and she'd fallen asleep smiling. She never questioned his absence earlier in the evening. She'd long ago stopped asking him where he went.

On Sunday, he'd detailed the car carefully. He casually mentioned to her that he was thinking about trading it in for another. She'd been so happy he was at home that she only smiled and said, "Whatever you want, dear." She was so easy.

With his alibi set, he was able to relax a little. Still, he scanned the paper for new developments and was pleased to find that the investigation appeared to be stalled. To be on the safe side, though, he stayed at home in the evenings and made sure she was happy. It was tedious work, and he wondered how much longer he could continue.

She was starting to talk about having children again, and he wasn't at all interested. He'd seen what having kids did to the guys at the office. Not to mention what it did to their wives. The men no longer had time to go out on weekends. They spent all their time going to ballgames and ballet lessons. Not him.

The wives looked like fat cows for nine months and after the babies were born, some of them still looked like that. No thank you. He could still enjoy looking at her body even if he didn't love her; the very thought of making love to some woman with stretch marks and varicose veins made him nauseous. He'd only married her because it made it easier to fool around.

The other guys in the office were less suspicious once he'd gotten married. Most of them were faithful to their wives and assumed he was as well. He had to admit that he'd been attracted to her in the beginning. It had been easy to make love to her then. The inheritance she had received from her grandfather had only added to his pleasure.

The attraction hadn't lasted, though, and he'd soon looked for something new. He'd never told her about the vasectomy he'd had done immediately after their marriage. That would have been grounds for divorce on her part, and he couldn't have that.

It had been two weeks now, and he was extremely bored. She had never been happier. She wanted to make love all the time, and he was getting sick of being with her so much.

On Thursday, he traded the old car for a new Lincoln. When he came home, she fussed a little because he'd spent so much money. He just laughed and told her, "You know, you can't take it with you when you go." She'd pouted, but had willingly gone for a ride. She was so simpleminded. His last connection to Eleanor had been severed, and he was feeling safe.

She wanted to go by the store before they returned home. He waited outside and studied the women who came and went. Maybe one of them would be his next conquest. The little redhead that bumped into him was a good candidate. She blushed so prettily when he looked up and down her. She hurried away before he could speak to her, though. Oh well, maybe he'd see her again. Rosemount was a small town, and he was a very good hunter.

Eleven

Another week passed, and Greg was missing Connie even more. There was nothing new on the case, so he couldn't use that as an excuse to call her. He really wanted to ask her to spend Thanksgiving with him at his parents' home.

Saturday evening, he decided to call and ask. She'd had two weeks. Maybe she was ready to talk. The phone rang four times, and then her machine picked up. He started to hang up, but decided to leave a message. If she returned his call, then he would know for sure she was ready to talk.

"Connie, this is Greg," he said. "I've missed you terribly, and I just wanted to talk. Give me a call back if you're ready."

The light was flashing on her machine when she came in Saturday night. She and Erin had been to a movie and out to dinner. At dinner, Erin had asked if she'd spoken to Greg yet. Connie told her no, and Erin had shaken her head and changed the subject. When Connie dropped her off, she'd said, "I love you girl, but I think you're making a big mistake. Call that man when you get home!"

Connie punched the message button on the machine. There were three messages. The first was from Keith Thomas. He was sorry, but he was unsure when he would be able to get by to fix her door. The second was a salesperson. She fast-forwarded past that one to the third message.

Her heart leapt when she heard Greg's voice. She knew immediately that she was going to return his call. Picking up the phone, she dialed his number with trembling fingers. He answered after the first ring. She was breathless and unsure of exactly what to say. He didn't seem to be having that problem. He was obviously happy to hear from her and didn't bother to hide the fact.

"I'm so glad you called," he said. "I've missed you. I'm tired of being apart. I know we haven't known each long, but I've never been surer of anything. I know we belong together!"

Connie was laughing and crying. When Greg was done, she said, "I want to see you, too."

Before she could say more, he said, "I'll be right over," and slammed the phone down.

While she waited for him to arrive, she freshened her makeup and put some water on for coffee. Her heart was racing, and she kept looking out the front window, watching for his headlights.

Greg made record time. Luck was with him. Traffic was light, and his car ate up the miles.

He pulled into her driveway in just under 25 minutes. She had the door open before he was out of the car. He took that as a good omen.

Bounding up the steps, he pulled her into his arms. "We can talk later," he said as he bent his head to kiss her.

He kissed her long and hard. Her arms twined around his neck as she responded with equal passion. He pulled her closer and molded her body to his. He could feel her heart racing and knew his own was keeping time. He had not forgotten what it felt like to have her in his arms. Her fragrance filled his head and made his senses swim. She smelled as sweet as the Lady Banks roses in his mother's garden. He was reluctant to let go.

Connie felt as if she had come home. His arms closed around her, and she was enveloped in the very essence of him. She didn't resist when he pulled her closer. She was right where she wanted to be. She was flushed and breathless when he took his lips from hers. He held her tightly for another minute and then released her. He watched the gentle sway of her hips as he followed her inside.

Her lips were rosy and swollen from the intensity of his kisses. She felt as if her body was on fire. Her hands were trembling as she attempted to close the door behind him. He pushed her gently aside and closed it. She walked into the living room and sat on the couch. She wasn't sure how much longer her legs would support her.

Greg took a seat beside her on the couch. He was having a little trouble catching his breath. The passion he felt with her was new to him. No other woman had left him feeling this way. He reached for her hands. They were trembling, and he rubbed them gently. He put his hand under her chin and turned her face to him. *She is so beautiful*, he thought. He leaned over and placed a gentle kiss on her lips.

She slipped her hands free and stood up. "Greg, I'm not sure what you're expecting from me, but there are some things you need to know. I don't sleep around. In fact, I'm Catholic. Like other Catholic woman, I don't believe in having premarital sex. If that's what you're looking for, then I'm not the woman for you. I like you very much and I enjoyed our kisses, but that's as far as I'm willing to go. If this is something you think you can deal with, then we can continue to see each other. If not, then you might as well leave now."

Greg stood up. He looked grim, and Connie was afraid he was going to walk out on her. Instead, he reached once more for her hands. "I feel like I've been waiting for you for all my adult life. There have been other women. I won't deny it. When I was younger, I took it for granted that they would sleep with me. It wasn't until later that I realized what a mistake I'd made. I've had only casual relationships for the last five years. I know now that God was telling me to wait for you. I'm Catholic, too, and my faith is very important to me. I try very hard to practice the teachings of the Church. It isn't always easy, but I have found that it can be very rewarding. If you can accept the fact that I wasn't always the man I should have been, then I think we might have something very special here."

Connie was crying now, and he hugged her to him. He stood in silence as he held her. He was praying as he hadn't prayed in a long time. *Please Lord, let this woman trust me with her heart. I won't let her down.*

Connie raised tear-filled eyes to Greg. She, too, had been praying. *Thank you, Lord for bringing this man into my life.*

Pulling away, she motioned for him to sit. She brought some coffee in from the kitchen, and they sat talking until 1 a.m. When Greg left, he promised to see her at Mass the following morning. Connie went to bed with a full heart and slept soundly.

Erin raised her hand in greeting as Connie walked into church the next morning. Then her eyes widened in surprise as she saw the man walking behind her. "I see you took my advice," she said to Connie while winking at Greg. "It's about time."

Connie blushed, and then introduced the two. Greg was charming and laughed at Erin as she told him how she'd pressed Connie to call.

"Well, to be perfectly honest," he said, "I called first."

Erin rolled her eyes at Connie and returned to her seat with the choir. Connie led Greg over, and they sat behind her. All through Mass she was aware of him beside her. She felt his hand on the small of her back as he followed her from the pew for Communion. Again, she thanked God for him.

Mass was always special, but today it was even more so. She felt so complete with this man near her.

After, Mass she introduced him to other members of the choir. Russ Williams asked Greg if he could sing. Greg laughed and shook his head no. He thought he could learn, though, if Connie was willing to teach him. The others laughed, and Connie felt her face warm. The group often had breakfast together on Sunday, and they invited Greg to come along. He agreed willingly. It was a great way to learn more about Connie.

After breakfast, they walked around town enjoying the day. Most of the shops were closed on Sunday, and the streets were quiet. They sat on a bench in the park. They held hands and watched the squirrels play chase.

It was a cold, clear day. The sky was a beautiful azure blue with a few puffy white clouds floating by. Connie had not felt this content in a very long time. Greg was happy, too. After awhile, he broached the subject of Thanksgiving. "Connie, I'd really like for you to spend the holiday with me at my folk's house. My mom really wants to meet you, and I want you to meet her and the rest of my family. We're a pretty easygoing bunch, and I think you'll have a good time."

Connie looked at him. "I'd like that very much. I can't stay the whole day, though. I spent last Thanksgiving with Erin's family, and I'm sure they'll ask again. I'd like to spend part of the day there as well."

Greg nodded, "That'll be fine. Mom usually has dinner around four. I could pick you up about 3:30 if that's okay."

"I think that'll be fine," she said. "We had dinner around one o'clock last year at Erin's."

Greg followed her back to her house and waited while Connie changed into jeans and a jacket, and then they took a long walk through the woods.

It was getting dark when they returned to the house. Greg started a fire in the fireplace. They made some spaghetti for dinner and ate in front of the fire.

Later, they sat close on the couch and watched as the fire burned down to glowing coals. He was loath to move, but knew he needed to be going. She walked him to the door, and he kissed her. She was sweetly responsive, and he left longing for more.

Connie waved as he drove away and then went back inside. She cleared the dishes and started some laundry. She went over her lesson plans for the week and around eleven, went to bed. She said her prayers and fell asleep.

The dream came swiftly, and she awoke screaming. She got up and made herself a cup of tea and read for a while. She went back to bed around 3 a.m. and slept undisturbed for the remainder of the night.

Twelve

It was snowing when she awakened Monday morning, light flakes that melted almost as soon as they touched the ground. She drove carefully to school. It had to snow a lot harder than this for school to be canceled.

The snow excited the children, and it was hard for them to concentrate on their lessons. Connie did the listening exercises with them after lunch. In the back of her mind was the voice from her dream. What was so different about that voice? She wished she could recall it more vividly. Maybe then she'd stop dreaming about it. It stopped snowing just after lunch, much to the chagrin of the children. They'd been hoping for a snow day on Tuesday.

Tuesday dawned cold and dreary with the promise of sleet before dark. The clouds were angry and dark. A cold wind whistled through the trees and cut through even the heaviest of clothing.

Connie's class had Thanksgiving dinner, courtesy of her room mother. Most of the mothers came to dinner and took their children home early. Connie was glad. With only five children left, she was able to do lesson plans for the following week. The children read or played games for the remainder of the afternoon.

She stayed later than normal, taking down the decorations for fall and putting up the Christmas ones. She was engrossed in her work when the classroom door slammed shut. She gasped and whirled around. Greg was standing there with a sheepish look on his face.

"Sorry," he said. "I wanted to surprise you, not scare you half to death. The wind yanked the door out of my hand."

Connie laughed shakily and said, "It's okay. I was so involved in what I was doing that if you'd just spoken, I probably would have reacted the same."

"I had some free time and wanted to take you to dinner," Greg said. "How about it?"

"Let me finish up here and then I'd love to go. It shouldn't take me more than fifteen minutes." She motioned to her chair, and he came forward. When he was close, he pulled her close and kissed her. She blushed and pulled away from Greg.

She went back to what she had been doing, aware that he was watching her. She wasn't used to being watched so closely and was all thumbs as she hung the last of the decorations.

He tried not to make her uncomfortable, but he liked looking at her. He surveyed the room appreciatively. She must really love her work to put forth all this extra effort. The room was like Connie, warm and welcoming.

She had a reading corner in the room, complete with several small rocking chairs and a rug. Books were stacked neatly on a gaily painted shelf in the corner. He could see some old classics he'd enjoyed when he was young, *Illustrated Classics, Tom Corbett, Space Cadet*, and the *Hardy Boy Mystery*. She had *The Chronicles of Narnia* by C.S. Lewis, the *Little House Series* by Laura Ingalls Wilder, and *Grimm's Fairy Tales*. She seemed to have something for every child to enjoy.

Less than half an hour later, they were seated at Atwells. It was a small family restaurant run by a local couple. The

Atwells hadn't been in Rosemount long, but their place was well-established. They served three meals a day with limited choices. Their dinner specials were different each day.

Tuesday's special was smothered pork chops, steamed cabbage, and macaroni and cheese. Connie and Greg ordered the special and topped it off with warm apple pie and coffee. They talked a bit about the case.

"Eleanor's car was found at a mall in Charlotte. It's been towed to our garage and is being looked over carefully. Perhaps we'll find something useful. I visited the club in Charlotte, too, but no one there could remember anything helpful. They remembered Eleanor, but couldn't identify her latest friend."

Connie shook her head sadly. "I wish I could remember what it was about his voice that was so distinctive. I keep dreaming about it, but it's too vague."

After dinner, he followed her home. The temperature had dropped into the twenties, and the wind tore through the trees. The weatherman was promising snow again on Thursday. Greg told her he had to be at work at five the next morning, so she sent him home early.

When he was gone, she sat by the fire and made some phone calls. Erin had left a message earlier inviting her for dinner Thursday. She laughed when Connie said she would stay until 3:30.

"I'm guessing you've gotten a better offer for later," she said cheerfully.

"You guessed correctly," Connie responded.

"Well, I won't hold it against you if you promise to give me all the details later," Erin said.

"You've got a deal," Connie said.

"Do they have anything new on Eleanor's case?" Erin asked. "I haven't seen anything in the paper for almost two weeks now."

"Nothing that I've heard," Connie replied. She still hadn't told Erin that she had seen the murderer or that she'd been the one to find the body. Greg still insisted she keep this information to herself. She wanted to tell Erin so badly. She wasn't used to keeping things from her. She evidently was better at hiding things than she thought. Erin didn't seem to realize that she was being evasive.

They talked for an hour and a half more, and then Connie watched some TV. When she went to bed, Eleanor was on her mind, so it was no wonder she dreamed of her killer again.

The dream was a bit different this time. The killer was chasing her through the woods. He was calling to her, and she was afraid. He was getting closer and closer. She was panting, and her side was hurting.

She tripped on some wood, and he was upon her. Just as he reached for her, Greg appeared. They fought as Connie lay on the ground watching helplessly. She awakened before the dream ended and couldn't get back to sleep.

It was only 5 a.m., but she got up anyway. She didn't want to lie there tossing and turning. She made a cup of tea and watched the early news. The wind was still howling, and the weatherman gave the temperature as eighteen degrees. She shivered in her pajamas, turned the thermostat up, and then settled down on the couch and fell asleep.

Thirteen

The ringing of the phone woke her up. She was groggy and disoriented and didn't make it to the phone in time. She heard the machine pick up and then heard Greg's voice. More awake now, she rushed to get the phone. She heard the click just as she lifted the receiver. Disappointed, she punched the message button. His voice was cheerful as he wished her good morning. He had just called to say hello and to tell her he was thinking about her. Listening made Connie feel warm all over her body. He was so thoughtful. She tried calling him back, but he didn't answer either at work or at home. *He must be out on patrol*, she thought. She'd call him again later.

She spent the remainder of the morning cooking. She made two chocolate layer cakes, one for Erin's family and one for Greg's. She made a pot of stew and a pot roast. She put these in smaller containers in the freezer. She didn't feel like cooking most days, but she wasn't fond of eating out by herself all the time. Besides, she wanted to be able to offer Greg a home-cooked meal when he arrived. It didn't take anytime to make drop biscuits and a vegetable to complete the meal.

She put a load of laundry in the washer and had some lunch. After that, she cleaned her bedroom. She loved her room. Her furniture had been her grandparents'. The oak four-poster bed had been modified to hold a queen-size mattress. The oak dresser had four deep drawers and a huge oval mirror.

Her Grandmother's vanity was her favorite piece. She could remember both her Grandmother and her mother using it. Her Grandmother had embroidered the bench seat when Connie was little. She dusted and polished the pieces until they glowed with a warm golden sheen. She put fresh sheets on the bed and made it. Her Grandmother had made the ivory quilt on the bed as well.

Connie had painted the walls a deep cranberry color to set off the oak floors and the ivory hangings at the windows. Even with the dark walls, the room was still bright in the afternoon because of its large windows. She loved the way the room now looked. She put some throw pillows on the bed, ran the vacuum around the room, and she was done.

The bathroom off the bedroom had been decorated to match. She cleaned that as well. She was just finishing when she heard a knock at the door. She looked at the clock and was surprised to find it was after four.

As she went to the door, she wondered who was there. The knock came again just as she got close, and then she heard Greg's voice calling. Happily, she opened the door. A draft of frigid air whirled into the room with him as he came through the door. She closed the door quickly. She took his coat and offered to make a cup of coffee to warm him up.

"All in good time," he said as he reached for her. Covering her lips, he kissed her till she was trembling in his arms.

"I couldn't wait to see you today," he said. "I called this morning, but you must have been out. I didn't want to waste time on the phone, so I just drove out hoping you'd be home."

"I had a little trouble sleeping last night and was up very early. I fell asleep later on the couch and couldn't make it to the phone in time. I tried calling you back at home and at work."

"I was out on patrol when I called," he said. "I called you from my cell phone. I guess I'd better give you that number as well."

"That'd be nice," she said. "I can give you mine, too. Would you like some dinner? I've been cooking today. You can have your choice of beef stew, pot roast, or I can make something else."

"The roast sounds great. What can I do to help?" he asked.

"Would you like rice or potatoes with it?" she asked.

"I prefer rice, but it doesn't really matter," he responded. "I can eat just about anything. When I first moved away from home, some of my cooking attempts were pretty pitiful. I learned quickly, though, and I'm a pretty fair cook now. Even my mother appreciates my efforts."

"Wow," she teased. "Good looking and he can cook, too. You know you're every woman's idea of a dream man."

"I'll remember that when you get too uppity," he quipped.

They worked companionably together in the kitchen preparing dinner. The pot roast was tender and juicy, the rice fluffy, and they ate heartily. Greg was relieved to see that she wasn't one of those women who picked at her food. She had a great figure, and he liked seeing that she didn't starve herself trying to be too thin.

Greg left around midnight, and Connie went to bed. She prayed that her sleep would be undisturbed, and it was.

Fourteen

The snow was a soft white blanket covering the ground the next morning when she got up. She stood at the window looking out at the beauty of the day. The evergreens looked beautiful against a backdrop of cobalt blue sky and pristine white snow.

The birds were at the feeder this morning. They didn't seem to be bothered by the cold. She watched them for a while and then showered. She was going to Mass at 10:00 a.m. and she wanted to leave early because of the snow on the roads.

She dressed warmly in a long winter-white wool skirt and sweater, brown leather boots, and brown cashmere coat. Erin called around nine and offered to pick her up for church.

She arrived around 9:15, driven by her father. The four-wheel drive Jeep Cherokee handled the snow-covered roads with ease. Erin's dad and mom were pleased to see Connie. She had been like another daughter to them. They talked easily on the trip into church.

When Mass was over, they headed back to Connie's house. Erin and her parents waited for Connie to run in and change, and then took her home with them.

Connie helped prepare the dinner, and they ate around 2 p.m. The meal was delicious, but Connie ate lightly. She knew she would be eating again in a few hours. She helped Erin and her mom clean the kitchen, and then they visited until three.

Erin drove Connie home and stayed while she waited for Greg to arrive. She pumped Connie for details of the relationship, and Connie finally capitulated. She told her almost everything.

Erin was ecstatic. She wanted Connie to be happy, and she had a feeling Greg was the right man for the job. Connie's face glowed and her voice was laced with joy as she talked about him. Erin's heart warmed to see her so happy. Connie had been so down lately, and she knew she'd been having trouble sleeping. Maybe that would end now.

She watched as Connie scrambled around trying to decide what to wear. She finally settled on slim black jeans, a black-and-gray-striped turtleneck, black leather jacket, and boots. She fussed with her hair and makeup, and Erin knew she was nervous about meeting his parents. She looked gorgeous when she was ready, and her eyes were bright with happiness. Erin thought she hadn't looked that way since before the death of her folks.

Greg arrived promptly at 3:30 and was greeted by Erin at the door.

"Happy Thanksgiving," she hailed as she ushered him into the house.

He smilingly returned her greeting. Connie came rushing into the room, carrying the cake she had baked. She didn't want Erin to have time to conduct "the inquisition." Aware that Erin was watching them, she hugged Greg briefly and practically pushed him out the front door. They both laughed at her obvious maneuvering, and she blushed. Hugging Erin, she whispered in her ear, "I'll call you later with details."

Erin was still laughing as she waved good-bye. She watched them drive away and said a little prayer for them.

Connie sat with the cake on her lap. She was quiet, deep in thought. She was a bit nervous about meeting his family. She wanted them to like her, and she wanted very much to like them. Family seemed very important to Greg, and she wanted to make him happy.

She prayed they'd like her.

Greg could see that she was apprehensive. He kept his mind on his driving and left her to her thoughts. The road was slippery from the snow that had melted and required both hands on the wheel.

Blue Springs was forty-five minutes from Rosemount and sat at the foot of a small mountain. The small, picturesque town was named for the spring that fed its water system. Mom and Pop stores lined Main Street, most of which were closed for the holiday. There were two traffic lights and very little traffic.

Connie was enchanted by the place. It looked like a Currier& Ives postcard. The snow had been heavier here and was mounded up on the side of the roads. Greg turned off Main Street and followed a winding road through the country.

His parents' place was about fifteen minutes outside of town. He made a left turn onto a small blacktop road. Five minutes later, he pulled through the gates of his childhood home.

Two large stone lions guarded the entrance to the drive, and a tall black iron fence ran along the front of the property. The driveway was long and winding. A canopy of tall trees blocked the sunshine as he drove.

Around the last curve, Connie let out a gasp of surprise as the house came into view. The red brick house was three-stories high, with large mullioned windows along the front. Tall columns stood on either side of the small porch before the front door. Connie thought it was beautiful. There were several cars parked in the area near the front door, and Greg pulled in behind them. He turned to Connie.

She was gazing around, obviously entranced. The yards were beautiful and well-tended. The house was huge, and she liked the way it sat on the grounds. It had a lot of character, at least from the outside. She'd had no idea what to expect. She'd managed to quell the butterflies in her stomach on the way over, but they returned now in full force. She looked at Greg and swallowed hard. He was watching her with a tender look in his eyes. She felt better instantly.

"They're going to love you as much as I do," he said.

"Thank you," she responded.

Leaning over, he kissed her softly and then got out of the car. Before he could open her door, the front door of the house swung wide and his brother James shouted, "Are you two going to sit outside all day? I'm hungry and dinner's getting cold."

Greg ignored him and helped her from the car. He carried the cake she'd made and put his arm around her shoulders. James was waiting as they walked to the door.

"If that's dessert, you can give it to me, especially if it's chocolate," he said. "Hi, Connie. I'm James, his good-looking older brother. Welcome!"

Connie smiled and held out her hand. "It's very nice to meet you. Greg talks about you a lot."

"Well don't believe most of what he tells you. I'm really a very nice guy," he said shaking her hand.

Connie was laughing. She was feeling more at ease already. She watched as Greg whacked his brother on the back affectionately.

"Come on, honey, and meet the rest of the family. They're not nearly as loud as James," he said. He took her hand and led her into a large living room.

The room was noisy and full of people and laughter. Greg looked around for his mom and dad. He spotted his dad near the fireplace and led Connie over to him.

Greg's dad looked up and smiled. Connie could see the love he felt for his son on his face. The two men hugged, and then Greg introduced Connie.

Mr. Reed was a mature version of his son. Tall and handsome, his brown hair was shot through with silver. He gave Connie a hug and welcomed her to his home.

A tall, slim, elegantly dressed woman hurried into the room. Her brunette hair was pulled back onto a soft chignon, and her makeup was flawless. *Not that she needs much,* Connie thought. She was beautiful. Her large green eyes were thickly lashed. Her full mouth was parted in a welcoming smile. Her ivory skin was tinted faintly with rose, and she walked like a model. She wore slim, brown pants and an ivory blouse. A pink cameo pin rested on the collar of the blouse. She hugged her son and turned to greet Connie.

"Welcome dear," she said in a warm, well-modulated voice. "I've been longing to meet you. Greg has spoken of you often these past few weeks."

Connie was reassured by Mrs. Reed's gracious welcome and relaxed. Greg took her around the room and introduced her to the rest of the family. His brother John resembled his mother, with those same green eyes. He was quieter than James was, but just as nice. His wife Marjorie was tall and slim with wide hazel eyes and a soft full mouth. His sisters, Carron and Patricia, were quite a contrast. Carron was tall and willowy. Her dark brown hair fell down her back in soft waves. Her eyes were large and dark brown. She moved in that same graceful manner as did her mother. She was soft-spoken like John and welcomed Connie warmly.

Patricia was petite, with short, curly auburn hair. Her topaz eyes were alight with humor as she, too, welcomed Connie. Her husband Daniel stood beside her with his arm around her shoulder. Connie saw him look lovingly at his petite wife as she talked.

Carron's husband was absent from the gathering. Her eyes were sad as she told Greg that he was working. Although Greg's mouth narrowed, he said nothing. It was obvious to Connie that he wasn't fond of his brother-in-law. James's wife Jenny was blond and petite, with a quick flash of humor in her blue eyes.

The children ran in from outside when the dinner bell rang. Their ages ranged from two to fifteen. They were boisterous, happy children. James had three children: two boys, Matthew fifteen, John thirteen; and a daughter, Elizabeth, who was ten. John's son Andrew was twelve, and his daughter Mary, ten. Patricia's children were younger. Her daughter Sarah was six, and her son Noah two. Noah blew noisy kisses at Connie when she smiled at him. He looked like his mother. Sarah was quieter, like her father.

The dining room was large. The walls were a warm ivory, and a large oriental carpet covered the wooden floor. A large cherry hutch sat against one wall, and a matching buffet on the opposite one. A crystal chandelier lit the room beautifully. A gleaming cherry dining room table ran the length of the room. It was large enough to seat twelve comfortably. A smaller table had been set up for the children.

Connie took her place between Greg and Carron. They held hands as grace was offered. There was enough food to feed a small army—turkey, ham, roast beef, stuffing, potatoes, and a varied assortment of vegetables. The soft parker-house rolls and sweet butter practically melted in her mouth. Conversation was lighthearted, and laughter filled the room.

Connie was enjoying herself immensely. They were such a loving family. The children were well-mannered, but not severe. They laughed and joked with each other as they ate their dinner. Only Carron seemed a bit sad. She chatted with Connie, but looked often at the empty space where her husband should have been. "We've been married for ten years now, but he's gone so often it feels as though we're newlyweds."

Carron shrugged and went on, "We're planning to have children soon, once Robert's job settles into a more normal routine. I want my children to really know their father. I want them to have the kind of childhood I had. Mom and Dad were fantastic parents. They were always there for us. Robert is an attorney. He's with one of the largest firms in Charlotte. That's why he's away so much. I hate it, but he loves his job, and I don't want to be one of those wives who are always complaining. It's hardest when he misses family holidays."

She smiled sadly and told Connie that it made her appreciate him more when he was at home. Dessert was to be served later, and Connie was thankful. She helped clear the table and clean the kitchen. They all treated her like one of the family. She saw Greg's mother giving her speculative looks as she dried the dishes.

Carol Reed was wondering if this would be her new daughter-in-law. She liked what she'd seen so far. Connie made her son happy and that was important to her. She vowed to get to know her better. She'd watched as Greg cut a swathe through the women in town for the past several years. Only one of them had even gotten close before Connie.

Greg had dated Irene Lawton for nearly a year. He'd been close to proposing when she told him she didn't want children. She loved him, but she wasn't giving up her career to raise kids. Greg had been devastated. He'd changed overnight. He started working all the time and rarely dated after that. Connie had changed all that in just a week. Carol was glad her son seemed to be getting back to his old self. She offered Connie a tour of the house when the dishes were finished. Connie accepted eagerly.

She had seen the rooms downstairs except for the master suite. It was decorated much the same as the dining room, with cherry furnishings, ivory walls, and another oriental carpet.

The bathroom held a large garden tub, a separate shower large enough for two, and a double vanity. It was decorated in pale blue and ivory.

There were four more bedrooms upstairs and a large sitting room, complete with a wide screen TV, a stereo system, and a computer. Two large comfortable couches and numerous chairs filled the rest of the room.

The third floor was a game room, complete with pool table and toys for the children. Carol told Connie they'd moved here when Greg was five. "Before then, we lived in a small house in town. My husband James became a partner in his father's law firm that year, and we used the bonus money for a down payment."

The time passed too quickly for Connie. They had dessert at 7 p.m., and everyone raved over her cake. She laughed and said, "Betty and I thank you." Greg looked confused, and Connie explained, "You know, Betty Crocker."

They all laughed, and Greg smiled at her. He wasn't sure what he'd done to deserve her, but he certainly was thankful. His family had adopted her as quickly as he had. They left at ten. Both his parents hugged Connie and urged her to come back soon. As Greg drove her home, he was filled with contentment.

Connie was quiet on the drive home. She'd had a great day and didn't want it to end. When Greg walked her to the door, she invited him into the house. They sat on the couch and talked quietly. She laid her head on his shoulder and sighed.

"Why the sigh?" he asked.

"I was just thinking how perfect the day was," she said. "I wish it didn't have to end."

"There'll be lots of days like today," Greg assured her tenderly, stroking her hair.

He lifted her chin with his finger and kissed her. She was breathless when he finally raised his head. His next words caused her heart to leap. "I love you, Connie," he said quietly.

"I love you, too," she said shyly.

Greg smiled. He felt as if he could take on the world right now. Everything in his life was finally falling into place. They sat for a time without speaking, each absorbing the impact of the words that had been spoken. When Greg heard the clock chime, he was surprised to find it was after one in the morning. He had to work tomorrow and knew he needed to get some sleep. He didn't like to be groggy at work.

"Honey, I need to go. I have to be in by 8 a.m. tomorrow. I guess that'd be today now," he said jokingly.

"Oh Greg, I had no idea you had to work the early shift," she said remorsefully. "I'm so sorry I kept you here so late."

Laughing, Greg shook his head. "I wanted to be here. I can work with five or six hours of sleep. That's about all I normally need. Stop feeling guilty. I wouldn't have left any earlier unless you had to go to work tomorrow."

They shared another long kiss, and then he left.

Fifteen

Connie slept wonderfully well and awakened remembering Greg's words of love. She and Erin were going shopping today, as they always did the day after Thanksgiving. There would be great sales at most of the major stores in Charlotte. She dressed warmly in jeans and a bright, yellow sweater.

It was another cold, clear day. The snow had melted, and the roads were clear. She smiled as she drove to Erin's house. She tooted the horn, and Erin emerged smiling. In Charlotte, they shopped for several hours. Around 2 p.m., Erin said, "I'm starving and I'm running out of money. Why don't we get some lunch now? We can shop more later if you like."

Connie agreed. They left the mall and twenty minutes later they were sitting in a booth at Hops. This was their favorite place to eat in Charlotte. The menu carried a wide range of food, but Connie's favorite was the Jamaican Top Sirloin.

She ordered the steak, a house salad with bleu cheese dressing, and steamed broccoli with garlic butter. Erin ordered the chicken pasta and a salad with garlic ranch dressing. The waitress brought their iced teas and some honey butter croissants. They nibbled on these while they waited for their salads to arrive.

"So," Erin asked, "How was it? I waited for you to call last night with those promised details, but I finally fell asleep around midnight. I've been extremely patient today, but now I want to know everything."

Connie grinned. She had indeed been patient. Erin didn't like to wait, and she always wanted details.

"It was wonderful," she responded. "They treated me like one of the family and were all so nice. The kids were so cute, especially little Noah. He's two, and I fell in love when I saw him. Greg's mom and dad were both so nice, and they invited me to come again soon."

The waitress brought their salads, and they were quiet for a time. Connie told Erin about the house, and Erin raised her eyebrows speculatively. "Hmm, sounds like there might be some money in that family. Does Greg have a single brother?" she asked half seriously.

"Erin, you know money is the last thing on your mind when you're looking for a guy. We both know that looks are more important," Connie teased. "And no, both of his brothers are married."

"How about a cousin then? I'm not choosy," Erin quipped.

They were laughing so hard they could barely eat. The waitress refilled their tea glasses and removed the empty salad plates. They managed to quell their laughter and finish the meal.

"That was delicious, as always," Erin said. "How long do you suppose it will be before Hops comes to Rosemount?"

Connie laughed. Rosemount was home to very few restaurants, and they were all small, family-owned businesses. They'd only just gotten their first hamburger place in July. "I think it's going to be awhile yet," she said. "Rosemount is too small to support a large restaurant."

They sat talking for a bit longer. The waitress brought the check, and Connie paid for lunch, leaving a generous tip. It was as they were finishing their tea that the dark-haired man walked past the table.

He was having lunch with his wife at Hops. He wasn't fond of the place. It was too quiet for his tastes. On his way to the bar, he spotted the two women at the table near the front of the restaurant. Good looking, both of them. Maybe he'd stop and chat on his way back to his wife. She probably wouldn't notice, and if she did, he'd tell her they were clients of his.

He flirted with the bartender while she poured his beer. He did enjoy the beer here. It was brewed on the premises and was some of the best he'd ever tasted. Carrying his drink, he wandered back to the table where the two women sat.

He stopped and looked them over appraisingly, smiling all the while. His eyes widened when he recognized the redhead who'd bumped into him outside the store. *Fortune was smiling on him today*, he thought. She was quite a doll, although her friend was more to his taste.

"Ladies," he said, in that gravelly voice that never ceased to make women long to hear more. "How are you doing today?" He was watching the tall one as he spoke and missed the way her friend suddenly paled.

"Can I buy you a drink?" he asked smoothly. He looked over at the redhead and noticed that her hands were shaking and she was very pale. He wondered what was wrong with her.

Connie couldn't believe she was hearing the voice that'd haunted her dreams for the last month. His voice was low and rough, at odds with his dark good looks. Her hands were shaking, and she clasped them together in her lap when she noticed him looking at them. She was sure her face was chalk-white. She was cold and her heart was racing in her chest. She kicked Erin under the table, and Erin looked over startled.

Erin couldn't believe how pale Connie was. What in the world was wrong? She'd been fine a minute ago. "What's wrong, Connie?" she asked, her voice full of concern.

Connie managed to pull herself together and say, "I'm okay. It's just a headache coming. We'd better get going while I can still drive. Excuse us please," she said sliding across the seat and exiting the booth.

She brushed quickly past the man, and hurried outside, not even looking to see if Erin was following. She was afraid she was going to be sick. That awful voice was filling her head. She swayed and leaned against the restaurant's wall. A hand on her shoulder startled her, and she looked up apprehensively.

Sixteen

Erin followed Connie as she made her way outside. Something was very wrong despite what she'd said. Connie never had headaches. Erin did, though, migraines that made her sick and unable to see for hours at a time. She controlled them with medication, and it had been a while since she'd had one. She watched as Connie leaned against the wall. She put her hand on Connie's shoulder, and her voice was rough with worry when she asked again, "What is it, Connie?"

Connie was crying now, and her whole body was trembling. She tried to answer, but couldn't. Erin put her arm around her, and they walked slowly to the car. She sank helplessly into the passenger seat.

Erin slid behind the wheel and took the keys from Connie's purse. She started the engine and turned on the heat. She watched carefully as Connie struggled to compose herself.

The heat in the car helped her to stop trembling. The coldness that had invaded her dreams this last month had returned at the sound of that voice. She knew Erin was worried and tried to pull herself together. She was able to speak after a few minutes more.

"That voice was the one I heard the night Eleanor was killed," she said faintly.

Erin was more confused than ever. *What was she talking about?*

Connie realized as soon as she said it that Erin didn't have any idea what she was talking about. How was she going to explain?

"What do you mean, Connie?" she asked. "What voice are you talking about?"

"The man in the restaurant. He's the one I saw on the road where they found Eleanor's body. At least his voice is the one I heard. I didn't get a good look at his face, but I haven't been able to forget that voice." Connie shuddered as she spoke.

"I'm still confused. You never told me any of this," Erin said accusingly.

"I wanted to tell you, but I couldn't. The police told me not to. They were hoping I could help identify the man and didn't want me to compromise the investigation. I've been very little help up till now, though."

Erin was shaking her head. "I can't believe you kept it from me all this time. I thought I could read you like a book. I never even imagined that you knew anything about Eleanor's death. Are you sure that man was the one you saw?"

Connie spoke softly, "I'm only sure of the voice, not the face. I need to talk to Greg. Will you drive me to the station in Rosemount?"

"Of course I will. I'm sorry I fussed. I know you would have told me if you could have. Do you think I should go back in and try to get his name from the hostess?"

"No," Connie cried. "If he's the man I saw, he might be a murderer. Greg will know what to do. I'm going to call him now. She dialed his cell number with shaky fingers. He didn't answer, and she was unsure about leaving a message.

She called the station, too, but was told he was not in his office. *He's probably off duty by now*, she thought. He'd gone in early today. Maybe she should try to find out the man's name. Even as she thought that, she noticed he was standing by the door looking out at them. No way was she going back into the restaurant. The police could handle it.

"Let's get out of here," she said to Erin. Erin nodded, and they left.

Seventeen

He wondered what had upset the redhead. She'd certainly been in a hurry to leave. Maybe he could help and in the process get some new numbers for his black book. He followed slowly, giving them time to get outside. He waited while they walked to the car. When he saw the car they got into, his blood ran cold.

It was a late-model black Ford Mustang. *It couldn't be the same woman*, he thought. What were the chances she'd been the one to see him the night of the murder? He was standing there stunned when his wife tapped his arm. He jerked and pulled away from her.

"Honey, are you okay?" She asked in her too sweet voice.

"I'm fine," he said roughly. "Let's get out of here."

"But I haven't finished eating yet," she said, perplexed.

"Well, finish without me. I'll wait in the bar."

He strode away, leaving her staring after him. He was too worried to care. He had some thinking to do and needed another drink, a stiff one. He ordered a double bourbon and drank it down in one gulp. He had to decide what to do. He'd heard her friend call her Connie. He knew she either lived or worked in Rosemount since he'd seen her at the store there. She wouldn't be too hard to find. He felt a tentative hand on his shoulder and turned. His wife was standing there.

"I took care of the check," she said quietly. "I'll finish eating at home."

He threw some money on the bar for the drink and followed her outside. The black car was gone, and he felt cold as he drove home. The new Lincoln ate up the miles, and soon they were back in Rosemount. He dropped her at home and, to her dismay, left again.

He needed to find the woman. He needed to know who she was and how much she'd seen.

Eighteen

She watched as her husband left. She sat at the vanity in her bedroom, thinking about her life. She had fallen in love with him the first time she'd seen him. His smile had sent chills up her arms, and the look in his eyes had made her vibrantly aware of her femininity. She had been unable to resist the attraction she felt. She'd known about his numerous affairs. Her father called him the playboy of the firm. Divorce was his specialty, and he was very good. She'd wanted to go out with him despite his bad-boy image.

Their first date had been incredible. They had gone to dinner at a very expensive restaurant in Charlotte. They had danced after dinner, and she'd had more to drink than usual. She'd been lightheaded and giddy with happiness.

She'd seen the other women looking enviously at her. She'd known that they were wishing he were their date. He'd insisted on walking her to the door when he dropped her off at the house. She'd been loathe to have the evening end and invited him into her home.

She lived in a small apartment in Charlotte at the time. He'd cajoled her into having another drink with him, and they'd ended up in bed. She'd been a virgin still. She had always taken her faith seriously and wanted her husband to be her only lover. He had laughed when she told him and said she needed to live a little first. She'd wanted to please him and had given in to him. It had been wonderful.

She'd awakened alone the next morning feeling guilty and happy at the same time. She'd waited anxiously for him to call all that day and the next.

Ten days passed, and still he hadn't called. She'd been depressed and was sure she was pregnant. She'd finally worked up her courage and called him. He was distant on the phone, but had agreed to see her that evening. He'd wanted to make love as soon as he arrived, and she'd given in once more. Maybe he'd be easier to talk to afterwards.

It hadn't been easy. He'd tried to convince her to abort the baby. He'd stormed out when she refused. She had cried for days and hoped he would call. He hadn't.

After a month, she'd gone to the doctor. Not the one she normally went to, though. She hadn't wanted to explain her pregnancy to him. He attended the same church she did and knew her family well. She hadn't wanted to see the disapproval in his eyes. The pregnancy test had been positive, and she'd decided for the sake of her child to move on with her life.

With her decision made, she'd been happier. She'd known it would be difficult raising a child alone, but was sure she could do it. Two weeks later, she lost the baby. She'd been devastated. She'd felt lost and alone once more.

Her family wondered what was wrong, but she had been unwilling to tell them. She'd been having dinner in town when she'd seen him again. Despite what he'd put her through, she was still attracted to him. He'd seen her, but had not come over then.

She had been dancing with her date when he approached. He'd cut in, and she had been deliriously happy to be in his arms once more. He had undressed her with his eyes, and she'd been unable to resist the pull of his smile.

She'd left her date at the restaurant and gone home with him. He'd never mentioned the baby, and she hadn't either. They dated continuously for several months. She'd been shocked when he proposed marriage. She'd said yes immediately. She hadn't wanted him to have time to change his mind.

The wedding had been arranged quickly, much to her family's dismay. They hadn't liked him from the start. She hadn't cared. She'd never been happier. That happiness hadn't lasted beyond the first year.

He'd changed law firms, and she saw less and less of him. He was always out with clients late at night. She'd tried to fool herself into believing his stories, but had finally stopped asking him where he went. It had been easier that way. She loved him deeply and realized that she wasn't going to change him. He'd refused to even consider having children, and she'd stopped pressing the issue after five years. She was lonely and unhappy. She'd made her bed and now she was dying in it.

Lately, though, things had been different. He had been coming home early and staying home at night. Even the weekends had been wonderful. He'd been so attentive, and she gladly accepted the change. They made love often, and he was as passionate as he'd been when they were first together. She was happy at last. Maybe he was finally changing.

She looked into the mirror and wondered whom she was kidding. He hadn't changed. Today, he'd been his old self again, and here she was sitting alone and wondering who he was with now. He hadn't known, but she'd seen him stop at the table and talk to the women. She hadn't been able to see them clearly, but she knew at least one of them was his type. It was starting all over again. Perhaps it was time to call a lawyer…and their accountant.

Nineteen

Connie spoke little on the trip home from Charlotte. Erin drove, but kept giving Connie worried looks. Connie was still so pale, and her hands were still shaking. She kept them clasped tightly in her lap; so tightly the knuckles were white.

Erin was worried about her friend. She pulled into the police station and killed the engine. "I'll go in and see if he's here," Erin said. "He can come out and meet you. You're still too shaky to be walking."

She left Connie sitting in the car and hurried into the station. Greg was in his office, and she didn't bother to knock. She burst in and told him what had happened. His face was grim as he followed her out to the car.

He threw open the door and knelt beside Connie's seat. "Sweetheart, are you okay?" he asked.

Connie started crying again, and he put his arms around her. He held her until her tears diminished and she was able to speak. "I'm sorry Greg. I didn't mean to fall apart again. Hearing him just brought it all back. Finding the body, Eleanor's funeral, and all those terrifying dreams that I've been having. I'm not usually such a crybaby." She wiped the tears from her eyes and sat upright.

"It's okay, darling," he said tenderly, "but I need you to tell me everything that happened today. Maybe it will help us catch this guy. Let's go inside where it's warm." Once inside, he fixed the two of them coffee and made them comfortable in his office.

He called the Charlotte police and asked them to send an officer to the restaurant to try to get some information about the man that Connie had seen. Many people paid restaurant tabs with credit cards. Perhaps they'd get lucky.

He brought in a recorder to tape the statements they were going to give. He wanted a statement from Erin as well. Maybe she would be able to give a better physical description of the man.

Erin watched the gentle way he tended to Connie, his love for her obvious. She loved Connie dearly, and she was happy that she had found someone like Greg.

Erin was unable to remember anything unusual about the looks of the man at Hops. She did, however, agree with Connie about the strangeness of his voice. It was easily recognizable. It was harsh and guttural and blatantly sexual, the kind of voice that would be appealing to some women. His eyes had been cold, though, and his approach studied. Erin had never liked that kind of man.

The phone in Greg's office rang twenty minutes later. The restaurant bill had been paid with cash, and though the waitress remembered the man and his companion, she didn't know their names. She was fairly new to the job and couldn't remember waiting on them before. Greg was intrigued to find out that he'd been with a woman. Maybe the waitress could give a description of her. He planned to go to Charlotte himself as soon as possible.

When they finished at the station, Greg followed them home. They dropped Connie's car at her house and then took

Erin home. When Erin offered to spend the night, Connie acquiesced. She knew she wouldn't sleep and the company would be nice. Erin was going to take a nap and come over after dinner. She figured she'd be up most of the night with Connie. She wondered if Greg would stay also.

Greg was planning to stay. With Erin there, he felt he could stay without compromising Connie's reputation. He didn't want her neighbors to start talking. It was a small town, and it was hard to keep some things quiet. His car parked in her drive overnight would eventually cause talk. He was going to protect her from that if he could.

Connie was feeling better now that she was home. Home had always been a haven. It was no different today. She visibly relaxed once she was inside. She could remember the man without trembling now. She wished she'd been strong enough not to run away from the man. She owed that to Eleanor.

She and Greg took a walk in the cold afternoon air. Back at the house, she sat at the kitchen table while he warmed some soup for dinner. She wasn't hungry, so she watched him eat. He made her laugh with stories from his childhood. He was a good man.

Greg ate his soup and talked to Connie. He watched the shadows leave her eyes and was grateful for the gift of words. Erin arrived around 9 p.m., and they stayed up playing cards and talking until nearly four in the morning. Erin slept in the room Greg had occupied before, and Greg stayed in the smaller room that Connie used as an office.

Connie put fresh sheets on the sofa bed in her office for Greg. She was glad he was staying the night. She was sure she'd be able to sleep with him here. It was comforting to have a man in the house. She looked up as Greg came in from the bathroom. He smiled and hugged her before saying goodnight.

She looked in on Erin before going to her room and saw that she was already fast asleep. Connie knelt beside her own bed and prayed the Rosary. It was quiet in the house when she crawled into bed. Perhaps it was the trauma of the day or maybe the fact that Greg was there. Whatever the reason, she fell deeply asleep and slept like a baby until nearly eleven the following morning.

Twenty

Greg awakened around nine and got up. The house was very quiet. The girls were still sleeping. He had slept lightly, listening in case Connie cried out in the night. She hadn't and he'd been glad. She needed some rest after the events of the previous day. He made himself a cup of coffee and walked out onto the porch.

It was cold and cloudy. *It looks like it might snow any minute,* he thought. He sat on the porch and drank his coffee. He liked the cold and snow. It gave the world such a clean look when it was fresh. He was happy living here. He couldn't imagine living somewhere like Florida where the seasons seemed to be much the same. Wearing shorts in December did not appeal to him. His sister Carron loved Florida. She visited an old friend there several times a year.

Thinking about Carron saddened him. She had always been quiet as a child, but happy. She wasn't as outgoing as Patricia, but she was warm and loving. Since her marriage to Robert, she had become even quieter and there was sadness in her eyes that never left.

He hadn't liked Robert Westlake from the start. He was a charmer all right, but as shallow as a pond after a long dry spell. Greg was sure Robert had only married Carron for her money and her looks. He'd never bothered to really get to know her. She made excuses for his frequent absences from family outings, but Greg was sure he was cheating on her. He was certain Carron knew it, too. He had watched as she withdrew into herself as the years went by. Even at twenty-five, Greg had known that Robert was a bounder. The children his sister wanted never came. She wouldn't talk about that, though. She just smiled her warm smile and changed the subject.

He stood up and went back inside. He noticed that the front door was acting up again and decided to have a look at it while the girls were still sleeping. He could see that it was swollen near the bottom, but was unsure how to fix it.

He went back outside to the shed behind the kitchen and looked for some oil. Maybe if he oiled the hinges and rubbed some oil around the frame it would help. He found the oilcan hanging on a nail near the rear of the shed. There was more than enough for what he wanted to do. He put the can back when he was finished and returned to the house. He heard noises in the hall bathroom and assumed Erin was up. It was 10:45, but Connie's room was still silent.

Erin emerged from the bathroom. She could see down the hallway and into the kitchen. Greg was sitting at the table drinking a cup of coffee. She walked in and removed a cup from the cabinet. "Got enough for two?" she asked. "I don't function well without my caffeine in the morning."

Greg smiled and poured the aromatic liquid into her cup. She sniffed appreciatively and added cream. They were quiet as they drank their coffee.

Connie wandered into the kitchen and found them sitting there. She said good morning and noticed that Greg had put water on for her tea. She wondered how many other men were that thoughtful. She knew her father had been as well as her grandfather. That was one of the reasons she'd had such a hard time dating. They never quite measured up, until now. She was sure both her parents would have liked Greg. She fixed her tea and sat beside him at the table. He told her about working on the door.

"I'm not sure if it will help, but I figured it couldn't hurt," he said.

"It was sweet of you to try," she responded. "I think maybe a new door is what I really need. That one has been a problem for more than a year. Maybe Keith will be able to hang a new one for me soon. I'll give him a call on Monday. I hate to bother him on a holiday weekend."

Greg and Erin left soon after, and Connie spent the day doing some work around the house. It started snowing around 5 p.m., and it was still snowing when Greg called at 6:30. He'd planned to come back earlier, but there had been a major traffic accident and he wasn't sure when he'd be free. She assured him she was fine, and he said he'd call later.

The evening stretched long and lonely before her. She cleaned out her closet and bagged some old clothes for the church thrift shop. She took a shower and decided to go to bed early. She fell into a troubled sleep and was awakened around ten by the sound of a car door.

She lay in bed trembling. She never had callers this late at night, and Greg had said he would call before he came to see her. Who was out there? She strained to hear what was happening outside. She heard light footsteps on the porch and sucked in her breath. What if the killer had found her? What should she do?

Stop acting like a wilting female, she chided. *Get up and find out who is outside.* She slipped out of bed quietly and tiptoed through the house avoiding the boards that she knew squeaked. She peaked through the curtains on the front window and froze when she saw the shadow on the porch.

Twenty-one

She was reaching for the phone when it rang. She was so startled she screamed. There was a sudden pounding on the door, and she heard Greg's voice calling for her. Her hands were shaking so badly she could hardly unlock the door.

Greg heard the lock click and pushed his way forcefully into the room. Connie was standing there shaking so badly her teeth were chattering. She flew into his arms and leaned weakly against his chest. He heard sounds coming from her and thought she was crying. He forced her face up and saw that she was laughing.

Connie was laughing so hard she could barely breathe. She couldn't believe what a shrinking violet she'd become. She'd always considered herself a strong woman. When had she become such a wimp? True, she wasn't used to finding dead bodies and she thought she'd come face to face with a murderer, but still. Well, maybe she did have a right to be somewhat wimpy. Greg had a worried look on his face. He probably thought she was hysterical. She said, "I'm not having hysterics. Really I'm not," she reiterated when he looked dubious.

Greg was uncertain what to make of her laughter. He'd never intended to frighten her.

That's why he had called before he knocked at the door. He'd noticed that the lights were out and had figured she might be asleep. If she hadn't answered the phone, he'd intended to go back to his car and go home. When he'd heard the scream, his blood had turned to ice. He couldn't get into the house fast enough. She'd scared the hell out of him!

And here she was laughing! He was sure she was hysterical. "What in the world were you screaming about?" he demanded. He was feeling a little foolish now and wanted her to make sense of it all.

"Why was I screaming?" she asked imperiously. "Wouldn't you be screaming if you saw someone skulking around on your front porch? How was I supposed to know it was you? You said you'd call first. I thought you were the killer. I was getting ready to call the police. Wouldn't that have been a hoot?"

Greg looked at her sheepishly, "I guess I should have called before I got here. That was me on the phone. I didn't want to bother you if you were in bed. I saw that the lights were out and was just going to leave you a note on the porch. I had no idea you were such a light sleeper. I'm really sorry I scared you."

Connie put her arms around his neck and hugged him tightly. She was so happy he was here. She could see how much he cared. It was blatantly obvious in his every action. She was a lucky woman. *If only he'd stop scaring her*, she thought humorously.

Greg rained kisses on her face and neck. She was the sweetest woman in the world, and he loved her dearly. He pulled away and said, "I promise I'll call first next time, and I'll limit my skulking to office hours.

Connie started laughing again, and he joined her. She offered to make him a snack, and he accepted eagerly. He hadn't had time for dinner and was hungry. A rush of adrenaline tended to do that to him.

Connie fixed two ham sandwiches and a cup of decaf coffee for him. She sat at the table and watched him devour the meal. She loved having him here. She was hoping that he'd suggest staying the night. He didn't disappoint her. He offered, and she couldn't say yes quickly enough. She didn't care what the neighbors thought. She liked feeling safe, and he provided the security she needed.

She fixed the bed in the room Erin had occupied the night before while Greg showered. He still had clothes in the car from the previous night. Connie was sitting on the bed when he came into the room. She looked like an angel in her long white gown. He wanted badly to touch her, but resisted the temptation. He was going to be strong. She deserved that.

Connie watched him as he walked towards the bed. His T-shirt molded to the muscles that rippled across his chest. His hair was wet from his shower and dark stubble shadowed his chin. He looked thoroughly masculine, and she felt her breath catch in her throat. She understood why women found it so hard to wait. She wanted this man now.

She knew she'd better get out of the room before she threw herself at him. He'd been so good about keeping their touches fairly innocent. She wanted more than those innocent touches now. She had to leave. She could feel her will weakening with every passing second.

She stood up and bade him goodnight. He must have sensed her weakness because he gave her a brief kiss and then pushed her from the room. She knew she should be grateful, but felt aggravated instead. She went to bed in a huff.

Greg had seen the look on her face when he pushed her from the room. He knew she'd be grateful later, but that certainly wasn't what she was feeling now. He'd seen the look in her eyes and knew what she wanted. He didn't want it to be like that. The guilt would be hard for both of them to live with later. He could be strong.

He prayed before he fell asleep and asked God for the strength to be just that. His last thought before sleep was the look she'd given him when she left the room. It made him smile.

Twenty-two

Connie awakened to find the world outside a winter wonderland. The snow had continued to fall well into the morning hours, and it was deep on the ground. She looked at the clock beside her bed. It was 7:30, and she was wide-awake. She'd slept like the dead knowing he was in the house. No dreams had haunted her sleep either. She listened, but heard nothing from the other room. She'd wake him after she'd showered.

Greg was awake and heard the water running through the pipes. The old house wasn't quiet. The pipes creaked and groaned as the water flowed through them. He liked the sound. It reminded him of his childhood, and the small house they'd lived in when he was young.

He smiled as he pictured Connie in the shower. *You'd better stop thinking like that*, he told himself. He wasn't sure his resolve was that good. He got up and looked out the window. A world of white met his eyes. He loved it. The sound of running water stopped, and he went into the hall bathroom. He showered quickly and stood at the mirror and shaved.

On his way back to the bedroom, he met Connie in the hallway. She was already dressed, and he could smell the scent of roses that he had come to associate with her. She was dressed for church and, as usual, she was lovely. He leaned down to kiss her good morning. Her breath was sweet, and she was soft in his arms.

"Good morning, darling," he whispered in her ear. "Did you sleep well?"

Connie cheeks were rosy and she answered quietly, "Yes." She was remembering, too, clearly her thoughts of last night. His touch was wreaking havoc with her self-control.

She pulled away and slipped back to her room.

Greg watched her go and frowned. He'd wanted to talk to her about something, but he supposed it could wait until later. Going into the bedroom, he dressed for church.

She frowned at her reflection in the mirror. If she kept this up, she'd be spending all her time in confession. She had to gain control of her emotions. She waited until she heard him close the door of his room before going to the kitchen. She was watching the birds at the feeder when he came into the room. He waited for her to speak and when she did, he smiled.

"I'm sorry, Greg. I didn't mean to be rude, but I can't seem to think clearly when I'm close to you like that."

"It's okay, honey. I've been having a bit of trouble in that department myself. Why don't we talk this out later after Mass?"

Connie nodded. They left early for church. The snow would make driving more difficult. Greg drove, and she sat relaxed in the passenger seat. He was careful to compensate for slippery road conditions, and she felt good with him at the wheel.

Attendance at Mass was down due to the icy conditions of the roads. Even a few of the choir members were absent this morning. Erin was there, though, and she looked at Connie carefully, checking for signs of upset. She seemed relieved by what she saw in Connie's face and hugged her.

When Mass was over, the three of them returned to Connie's house. Greg wanted to talk to both of them. They prepared eggs, bacon, toast, and coffee, and sat eating at the kitchen table. He waited until they were finished before broaching the subject of the incident at Hops.

"I wanted you to both to know that I went over to Charlotte yesterday and talked to the waitress at the restaurant. Our man wasn't alone at the restaurant. The waitress couldn't remember much about his companion other than the fact that she was tall, slim, and brunette. It seems she paid more attention to the man. She said he flirted outrageously with her and the woman said little or nothing the whole time they were there. She was embarrassed by the attention and tried to stay away from the table as much as possible. The brunette paid the check with cash, and they both left before they finished eating. The waitress also said the woman seemed upset when they left, probably because the man had left and never returned to the table. She saw him again in the bar right before they left. We're waiting to talk to the bartender who worked Friday, but she's out of town until tomorrow. I'm going to interview her myself."

Erin was the first to speak. "Perhaps the bartender will remember something more helpful. If he tried to charm her, too, maybe she got his name."

"I can't believe I was so stupid. I should have stayed and talked to him. If only I hadn't been so frightened." Connie stood up and started pacing the kitchen. "It wasn't as if he was going to hurt me right there in the restaurant. I wish I'd been calmer."

"You did exactly what I would've done," Erin said staunchly. "I can't see myself sitting calmly, talking to a man I think murdered my friend. I probably would have run from the place screaming my head off."

"If you had tried to question him, he might have gotten suspicious and we'd still be right where we are now. At least he doesn't suspect that you recognized him," Greg said.

Connie remembered how he'd been standing watching them as they sat in them car and wondered if he had suspected something was wrong. She remembered, too, that she needed to tell Greg about seeing him outside the store. She was fairly certain it had been the same man. He hadn't spoken to her that day, but she remembered his smile and those eyes that had undressed her while she apologized. " I forgot to mention this on Friday, but I'm pretty sure I saw him once before. He was standing outside the market, here in Rosemount, one afternoon when I came out. I bumped into him. He didn't speak to me, but the way he looked at me made me uncomfortable."

Greg was excited when Connie told him about seeing the man in Rosemount. It narrowed the search pattern considerably if he lived here in town. Surely someone would remember having seen him with Eleanor and know who he was. It was the first solid lead they'd had in the case. Rosemount was small. He couldn't hide forever.

The three spent the remainder of the day together. They went for a walk through the snowy woods and had dinner in front of the fire. Erin left around 6 p.m., wanting to give them some time alone. She hugged Connie and Greg before she slipped out the door.

The Beast refused to crank, and she was forced to borrow Connie's truck once more. "I've really got to put this monster in the shop," she told them. "This is getting ridiculous. I never know where I'm going to be stranded next!"

Greg left around eleven. He spent the time on his drive home thinking about the case. He was going to Charlotte first thing tomorrow to talk with the bartender.

Connie spent a restless night with the killer hovering on the fringes of her dreams. She awakened listless and heavy-lidded.

The watery morning sun did little to lift her spirits. The temperature had plummeted during the night, and it was bitterly cold when she left for work. The snow was still thick on the ground, and the roads were icy. She drove slowly and still found herself sliding on patches of ice. She was even tenser by the time she arrived at school.

The day loomed long before her, and she was dreading it. She wished she'd called for a substitute. She hated feeling this way when she was working. The children sensed her mood and were strangely subdued. She saw the effect she was having on them and was even more depressed. They deserved better. She was going to take some time off if she wasn't feeling better by the end of the week.

It started sleeting around 5:30, and choir practice was canceled. Greg called and said he had to work late, so he wouldn't be able to see her that evening. She was almost relieved. She didn't really want him to see her in this condition anyway. She had dark circles under her eyes and couldn't seem to work up enough energy to smile. She took a sleeping pill around eight and went to bed soon after.

Greg arrived at the restaurant in Charlotte around lunchtime. He was planning to talk with some of the more experienced staff members as well as the bartender. Perhaps one of them would be able to give the killer a name.

The bartender was a petite blond named Joy. She was pert and bubbly, with a quick wit that made him smile. She remembered the man. It was clear by the way that she wrinkled her nose that she had been unimpressed by his charm. "I've been a bartender for twenty years and I've seen all types," she said. "His is by far the most despicable! He all but suggested I leave work and go straight to a motel with him. What a jerk!

You should have heard the way he snapped at his wife when she came to the bar. I felt so sorry for her."

"How do you know she was his wife?" Greg asked.

"Are you kidding? No girlfriend I know would let a man get away with garbage like that. It's a shame really. She was a very attractive woman. She could do lots better than that creep she was with. He was good looking, but his eyes were as cold as the grave, and that voice! Ugh! It was like sandpaper on silk."

"Did you happen to catch his name?" Greg asked.

"He didn't give it, and I wasn't interested enough to ask," Joy said. "Why are you asking about him anyway?"

"He's a suspect in a murder case I'm working on," Greg replied.

Joy's mouth fell open and her eyes widened. "I wish I could be of more help, but that's all I can tell you. If he comes back in, I could give you a call."

"We're working with the local police, so call them first. They'll let me know if you call."

She looked a little disappointed, and Greg wondered why. It became clear when she slipped a card with her phone number on it into his hand as he was leaving. He looked at her, surprised. "Hey," she said. "You can't blame a girl for trying."

He smiled and left the bar. Talking to the other staff proved fruitless as well. No one remembered the man or his wife. Apparently, they weren't frequent diners. He left disappointed.

He drove to the Charlotte police station and talked to the officer who had been sent to the restaurant on Friday. He, too, had learned nothing of value. When Greg left Charlotte around 3 p.m., he noticed that the clouds were thickening and it was getting colder. *It'll probably start sleeting before I get home*, he thought. He was right.

By the time he pulled into the station, the roads were icy and dangerous. He barely had time for a cup of coffee before he was called out on an emergency. There'd been a four-car pileup on I-40, and it took several hours to clear it up. He called Connie from the scene to say he wouldn't be coming over tonight. He could tell by the sound of her voice that she was feeling low. He wished he could be with her. It was after midnight before he dropped exhausted into bed. He fell asleep immediately and dreamed of Connie.

Twenty-three

He'd spent the weekend at a hotel in Asheville. He'd come up with a plan to find the redhead, but had to wait until today to put it into action. At 8 a.m., he called the office of Josephine Wilkins, PI. He'd never used her services before, but he had heard she was good.

He told her he was working on a bitter divorce case and needed to know the identity of the husband's mistress. He gave her the description of the woman and the make of the car he'd seen her drive away in that night. He told her he thought she lived in Rosemount or close by.

She agreed to take the case and told him she'd get back to him as soon as she had some information. He told her he was hard to reach and that he'd just check with her every morning around eight. He hung up feeling more confident. Soon he'd know who she was, and then he'd find out what she knew.

He returned home that evening and was surprised to find his wife gone. There was no note to explain her absence and that worried him. Perhaps he'd been too harsh with her on Friday.

He called her parents, but they refused to tell him anything. He slammed the phone down angrily. That witch had better get back where she belonged. She had no idea who she was dealing with! Maybe it was time to get rid of her, too. She'd become a liability these last few weeks. He poured himself a bourbon, and then another. When the phone rang shortly after nine, he was drunk and angry.

She'd asked the security company to notify her if the alarm system was shut down. They called around 6 p.m., and she knew he'd come home. She waited until just past nine before she called. She could tell he'd been drinking when he answered the phone.

He started swearing at her before she could say much. She waited for his tirade to end, and then she told him that she'd seen a lawyer and she wanted a divorce. He started shouting again and she hung up. She'd call tomorrow when he was sober. *Not that it would matter,* she thought. Her mind was made up. She went to bed.

Twenty-four

Connie awakened feeling better Tuesday morning. She had slept well after taking the pill and couldn't remember her dreams. She was thankful for that. The weather was still nasty and driving conditions were hazardous. Her cell phone rang as she was pulling into the parking lot behind the school. Answering it, she was happy to hear Greg's voice. "I'm so glad you called. I'm really looking forward to seeing you this afternoon. Yesterday wasn't a great day, but I'm feeling much better this morning."

Greg's call to Connie was motivated by concern and a need to hear her voice. He'd missed her, and he wanted her to know it. He was relieved to hear the upbeat tone of her voice. She sounded so much better today. He felt his own spirits lifting. They made plans to meet for dinner around five, and he hung up.

When her phone rang the second time, she was surprised. Erin's bubbly voice came over the line. "Hey," she said. "I made arrangements to have the beast towed into town this afternoon. Do you think you'll be home in time to meet the driver?"

"I just made dinner plans with Greg," Connie told her. "I can call and cancel if you need me to meet the driver, though."

"I was hoping you'd be there. I can't leave early today. We've got bigwigs from the state coming to look over the library accounts this afternoon and I have to be there. I was also hoping to use your car tomorrow instead of the truck. I have to take them to lunch, and we won't all four fit in the cab." Erin paused and sighed, "I know I'm a lot of trouble, but surely I'm worth it."

Connie was laughing as she assured Erin that she was indeed a lot of trouble. "I'll call Greg and tell him I can't make dinner. Maybe he'll come out to the house instead."

Erin thanked her and hung up. Connie dialed Greg's office number, and he answered after three rings. She explained the situation, and he agreed to come to the house instead.

"I'll bring dinner with me. I don't want you cooking again. It's my turn to feed you," he said.

Soon it was 3:30, and she was on her way home. She was still feeling refreshed and happy. She changed into jeans and a turtleneck and lounged around the house waiting for the tow truck. Pat's Towing Service was locally owned, and she recognized the driver as a fellow parishioner when he knocked on the door around 4:30. They chatted for a few minutes, and then he hooked the beast up and left. Connie waited on the porch for Greg to arrive.

He pulled into the yard at 5:45. He could see Connie sitting on the porch. Her cheeks were rosy from the cold, and her eyes were glowing. She came skipping down the steps as he got out of the car. He watched her thinking how much he loved her. She was the only woman for him. He'd already decided he wanted to marry her. He was just waiting for the right moment to ask her. He didn't want to rush things. He wanted them to be perfect.

He caught her in his arms and kissed her cold lips until they were as warm as the glowing embers he could see in her eyes. He retrieved their dinner from the car and followed her inside. They ate on TV trays in front of the fireplace. Connie had a roaring fire going, and it was toasty-warm in the house.

They had takeout from Atwell's: roasted chicken, stuffing, green beans, gravy, and dinner rolls. They polished it off in record time. Greg leaned back on the couch and sighed. "I'm stuffed. That was delicious. It was almost as good as my mother's cooking."

Connie nodded agreement. She leaned against his shoulder, and they watched the fire. Greg looked down at her face, rosy in the glow from the fire. He couldn't resist the temptation and leaned down to kiss her. She smiled and ran her fingers over his face. Her touch was tender. She kissed him and then stood up. He followed, and they cleaned up the dishes.

Later, in front of the fire, they shared more kisses. He hated to leave, but the time passed too quickly. She shooed him out at 9:30. She went to bed soon after and slept soundly.

Erin arrived at seven the next morning to pick up the car. They followed each other into town and went their separate ways. Wednesday was far warmer than Tuesday had been. The sun was shining brightly, and the temperature rose into the fifties. Connie took a walk during her lunch break enjoying the sunshine.

She went directly home after school, and Greg came over around five. She had cooked a nice dinner, and he was openly appreciative. He hugged her tightly and assured her, "You know even if you were as ugly as sin, I'd still date you."

She punched him in the arm and stuck her tongue out at him. The teasing turned to something more serious and soon they were both breathless. "We'd better take a walk and work off some of this excess energy," Greg suggested. Connie agreed. They bundled into their jackets and walked the woods for nearly an hour.

She made some coffee when they returned, which they drank with a piece of apple pie. Greg left at ten, and Connie picked up the house a bit before going to bed. She was surprised she hadn't heard from Erin about returning the car.

Twenty-five

She called him back on Tuesday to discuss the divorce. He pleaded with her to return home. He promised things would be different. She felt herself weakening when he told her he loved her. He hadn't said that in a very long time. She said she'd consider it, and he thanked her. She hung up confused and lonely. Why couldn't he be like that all the time?

She loved him as much as she ever had. The years hadn't changed that. Even his constant philandering hadn't been able to quell her feelings for him. What was wrong with her that she couldn't please him more? She'd tried. Lord knows she'd tried. What more could she have done?

She was still an attractive woman. She worked out regularly and hadn't gained even a pound since they'd been married. She knew how she looked was important to him. She had her hair cut and shaped every couple of weeks and had it highlighted when he mentioned how much he liked that.

She wore the clothes he liked even when they weren't to her taste. She preferred her skirts a bit longer and more conservative, but he liked looking at her legs. She'd given in to him. It hadn't been worth fighting over with him. Even the sexy lingerie she wore was for him. She'd never even considered not doing what he wanted. She loved him and wanted him to be happy. Maybe she should go home and try once more. What harm could it do?

Twenty-six

Jo Wilkins used her contact at the DMV to learn the name of the woman her client was searching for for his divorce case. She obtained other vital information as well. Address, phone number, car registration numbers, and driver's license number. She used other contacts as well and obtained more personal information.

She followed Connie on Tuesday and talked to some of her neighbors and co-workers pretending to be an investigator from the school board. She was a bit surprised by how popular this woman seemed to be with everyone. She didn't seem like the type to carry on a sleazy affair with a married man, but you could never tell what people in love would do. In her line of work, she'd seen it all. She typed up her report that afternoon and went home.

When her client called on Wednesday morning, she could tell he was pleased with her work. He was effusive with his gratitude and promised more work in the future. He asked what he owed and promised to send it immediately. She was grateful for that.

Her business had been slow lately, and she needed the work. Men were often leery of using a female investigator. Her reputation was good, and her contacts were growing, but still she needed more work. She was good at what she did and tried not to work too far outside the law. She went to lunch that day feeling good about the job she'd done.

Twenty-seven

Erin had a long day at work and was tired. She decided to stay in town for dinner.

She was planning to return Connie's car on her way home. She had dinner with a friend from work at a small Chinese restaurant on Main Street. It was eight by the time she left Rosemount.

Twenty-eight

He was elated by the information Wilkins had given him. The file she faxed over was thick and contained more information than he had expected. He now had her name, address, phone number, place of employment, marital status, and vehicle tag numbers.

The file listed the make and model of both vehicles she owned, listed her parents as deceased with no close relatives, and indicated that she lived alone. The file did contain two disturbing pieces of information. She had been a friend of Eleanor's and was currently dating a cop. That worried him. He wondered just how much she'd told her boyfriend.

Her address, too, gave him pause. She lived off of CR 358. He was sure now that she'd been the one who'd seen him that night. There was no other explanation for her reaction to him at the restaurant. He decided to drive by and check out her house. He waited until it was dark, then drove slowly by. He couldn't tell if her car was in the drive or not. It was too dark. The house was brightly lit, and he assumed she was home. He needed to think about what his next move would be. He drove by and turned around a mile up the road. He passed by again, but still couldn't tell if she was at home. He'd better get home. A few miles farther on, he met up with the black Mustang. *What an opportunity!* He hurriedly turned his vehicle around and soon caught up to the car. The tag number was hers.

Erin drove slowly on CR 358. The ice had melted earlier in the day, but was freezing on the road once more. She noticed the car that was creeping closer to her bumper. She slowed more, hoping they'd pass her. The jolt to the rear bumper shocked her. What was happening? Couldn't they see her lights?

The second hit infuriated her. She punched the gas pedal and pulled away from car behind her. She was mad, but she was scared, too. Her heart was racing, and her knees were shaking so badly she was having trouble keeping her foot on the gas pedal. She looked in the rearview mirror and was terrified to see the headlights looming closer again. She floored the gas pedal, and her tires slid on the icy pavement. She was rammed harder this time, and the steering wheel jerked from her hand.

The car hurtled off the road and into a deep ravine. The sound of grinding metal filled her ears as the car plunged down the sides of the ravine. She was praying now, her mind filled with thoughts of death. The car slammed into the trunk of a huge oak tree, and Erin was knocked unconscious.

The chance to rid himself of a potential menace was too great to ignore. The first hit was a warning. He wanted her to know she was going to die. The second was more serious. He was surprised by her sudden burst of speed. He'd expected her to panic and lose control. He was nervous now. He couldn't let her get away from him. He might not have another chance like this. He sped up and hit her hard.

He watched, relieved, as the car slid and plunged off the road. He didn't stop. If the accident didn't kill her, exposure to the elements would. It was supposed to be in the low twenties tonight. It was a lonely road with little traffic. Surely no one would find her before morning. Feeling better, he quickly left.

Erin wasn't sure how long she'd been unconscious. She was bitterly cold and couldn't move her legs. It was quiet and dark in the car, and her head was pounding viciously. For a moment, she couldn't remember what had happened, and then it all came flooding back.

Someone had forced her off the road. Were they trying to hurt her? She couldn't begin to imagine anyone trying to hurt her. She tried opening the car door, but it was jammed. She listened for sounds from the road above, but heard nothing. CR 358 was sparsely traveled, and she knew help would be slow in coming. Suddenly it occurred to her that no one would even know she was down here. She was too far off the road. She'd better try to help herself. She decided to wait a bit to see if the feeling would return to her legs.

She struggled to reach the blanket that Connie always kept in the back seat during the winter. It was several long grueling minutes before she was successful. She wrapped it around her legs, feeling for broken bones as she did. She couldn't feel anything, but she knew that didn't mean much. Maybe her legs weren't broken. Perhaps it was her spine that was injured. She shuddered thinking about it. *Pull yourself together*, she thought. *If you keep your head, just maybe you'll still be alive tomorrow. Maybe it was already tomorrow.*

She didn't have a watch, and the dash lights wouldn't work. She sat shivering in the cold, dark car, wondering how in the world she was going to get out of this. She must have drifted into unconsciousness again, because the sound of tires squealing on the road above jarred her back to reality. She began honking the car horn desperately, her hands almost numb from the cold. She prayed that someone would hear her cry for help.

Twenty-nine

Greg drove slowly, but was still caught off guard by the patch of fresh ice on CR 358. He tried to control the skid, but it was too late. The tires squealed, and he slid into the opposite lane before he was able to stop. He crossed the road slowly and pulled to the side. He opened his window for a breath of cold air. He was shaken up by the near accident and needed to clear his head.

He gulped in great breaths and tried to quiet the racing of his heart. He heard the sound of a car horn just as he was about to leave. He listened carefully, trying to ascertain where it was coming from. There were no other cars on the road that he could see, and he didn't hear any engine sounds. He got out of the car and listened again. The noise seemed to be coming from a deep ravine alongside the road.

Returning to his car, he retrieved the powerful flashlight that he always carried. He shone the light down the hillside, but could see little. It was so dark. The sound of the horn was quiet now, and he supposed it might have been coming from farther up the road. He returned to his car.

He was about to start the engine, when the noise resumed. He pulled the car back to the opposite side of the road and angled his headlights down into the ravine. He could see better now the signs of broken branches and small trees having been torn down.

He took the flashlight and started the steep descent into the ravine. He slid several times as he made his way down the slope. It was rough going. The sound of the horn stilled once more, but Greg still couldn't see anything. He prayed that he would get there in time.

Erin's head was still hurting, and she could barely muster the strength to sound the horn repetitively. She was so cold now, and it was becoming more and more difficult to make her hands do what she wanted. When she heard the engine again, she forced them to press harder against the steering column. She was so tired. Her eyes wanted to close, and she wanted to go to sleep. She knew she was weakening, and she was scared.

She prayed and asked God to forgive her sins and her last conscious thought was of her parents. She hoped they would always remember how much she had loved them. Her head fell to the side, and she slipped into unconsciousness.

Greg could just barely make out a large, dark shape at the bottom of the ravine. He slid the last few feet and realized that it was a car. It was badly mangled, and he thought it was a miracle anyone could still be alive in the tangled wreckage. He moved as quickly as he dared because he feared that time was running out for whoever had been in the car. He hurriedly pushed his way through the undergrowth and struggled to reach the driver's side of the vehicle. He shone his flashlight through the window and could see someone slumped behind the wheel. He tried the door, but it stubbornly refused to budge.

Going to the passenger side, he was able to open the door. He reached across the front seat and felt for a pulse. It was slow and breath sounds were shallow. He called for emergency aid with his cell phone. He looked at the victim and realized it was a woman. Long dark hair matted with blood fell over her shoulders. The blanket that was wrapped around her was blood-soaked as well. He lifted her head trying to get a look at the wound and was shocked to see Erin's face. At least he was pretty sure it was Erin.

Her eyes were closed, and her face was covered in blood. It was hard to equate the bloody mess in front of him with the vibrant face he was used to seeing. He brushed the hair away, and used a corner of the blanket to clear some of the blood from her eyes and cheeks. It was Erin! He knew he needed to try and warm her up until the rescue unit arrived. She was deathly cold. He climbed into the car and wrapped his arms carefully around her, not disturbing her too much. The cold from her body radiated into his and, before long, he was shivering.

The sounds of the sirens cut through the night, and he knew help was coming. He heard sounds from above and began shouting to them, telling them where they were. Erin's breathing had all but stopped now, and he was afraid she was dying. There was so much blood, and she was so cold. He wondered how long she'd been down here before he found her.

Bright lights shone into the car, and two paramedics helped him out of the vehicle. They took his place inside, and he watched with bated breath as they worked on Erin. They hooked up oxygen and started an IV after calling the hospital for permission. Two firefighters had carried a stretcher down, and they carefully lifted her from the car and placed her on it. She was pale and still. Greg began praying.

Thirty

Paramedic Blane Collins was sure the woman was going to die. Her pulse was too slow, and respiration was shallow and irregular. She had lost too much blood and was blue around the lips. He didn't think there was much to be done, but he would try his best to save her.

The veins in her wrist collapsed as he tried to put the IV in, and he was forced to try several times before he was successful. The oxygen mask covered her mouth and nose, and she looked small and helpless as they transferred her to the stretcher. His partner, Clay Winston, was shaking his head at the man who had been at the scene when they arrived. The stretcher was pulled back up the hill from above by the firefighters. The men climbed slowly behind, slipping on the rocky hillside as they struggled to keep the gurney stable.

CR 358 was brightly lit now and swarming with rescue workers, two rescue units, a fire truck, and several police cars. Blane's patient had stopped breathing, and her heart had failed. They began CPR and placed her in the unit. They continued CPR for several minutes before they were able to get a pulse. She stopped breathing twice more on the long trip to the hospital. He looked at Clay and shook his head. In the light of the unit, they could see that she had sustained a severe head injury. Blood loss was massive. It would be a miracle if she survived. He began to pray as well. He'd seen miracles before and that was what he was praying for now.

Greg followed the rescue unit to town. He called the station and was given the number of Erin's parents. He called them himself. They were shocked and afraid. He didn't tell them that she had stopped breathing at the scene. If she lived, it wouldn't matter. If she died, they would know soon enough. It was as he was dialing Connie's number that he realized it had been her car at the bottom of that ravine

The phone pulled her sharply from sleep. She answered it groggily, wondering who was calling at such a late hour. It was almost midnight. She was surprised to hear Greg's voice on the line. She could hear the sadness in his voice as he told her what had happened. She listened quietly then hung the phone up.

She jumped from her bed and dressed hurriedly. Greg was sending a squad car to pick her up and drive her to the hospital. In ten minutes, she was seated beside Mike Cook in his car. She was pale and quiet, and he didn't try to talk. When they passed the scene of the accident, Connie was horrified by the number of vehicles there. Her mind was whirling with thoughts of what must have happened. Erin was an excellent driver, if a little too fast. She must have lost control on the icy road.

She was praying as they pulled into the front entrance of the hospital. Greg was waiting for her there. He helped her from the car with a quick thank you to Mike, and they raced down the corridor to the emergency area. Erin's parents arrived within minutes, and they all sat huddled together in the waiting room.

The doctor looked grim when he came out a few minutes later. He spoke briefly, "Erin is on her way to surgery. She has sustained numerous internal injuries as well as severe head trauma. It is uncertain how long she might have gone without oxygen, and it will be some time before we'll know the full extent of her head injuries. At this point, that's all I can say."

Mrs. Sims collapsed at the news, and her husband and Greg carried her to a couch across the room. She was crying, and her husband was doing his best to comfort her. Connie was shaking and fighting to keep the tears at bay. Greg pulled her close, and she was thankful for his quiet strength. The doctor left, and they resumed their vigil.

The first light of morning was breaking the sky when the doctor returned to the waiting room. Dr. Hollis looked at the hopeful faces turned to him and felt his own heart sink. The news wasn't that good. "Erin made it through surgery, but it was touch and go. It could be days before we know anything for sure. Her injuries are so severe. She's in recovery now, and you can see her briefly once she's moved into Intensive Care." The doctor didn't want to offer false hope, but he wished he could have been more reassuring.

Mr. and Mrs. Sims left to call Erin's brother, and Connie and Greg went to the cafeteria for some coffee. Mike Cook was waiting for them when they returned from the cafeteria. "How's she doing?" he asked. Greg filled him in, and Mike offered to wait with them until they knew something more. They sat quietly pretending to read the magazines provided by the hospital auxiliary. At 6:30, Connie called and asked for a substitute teacher for the day. She knew she would be of no use to her children today.

At 7:30, Dr. Hollis came to get them. He looked grimmer than before. "Erin is in Intensive Care now, but she has slipped into a coma." Mrs. Sims collapsed again and had to be sedated. Connie wept quietly as the Dr. Hollis led them to Erin's room.

Erin looked small lying in the high bed with so many wires and tubes coming from her body. Her beautiful hair, which had been shaved in places for the surgery, was covered now with a large white bandage. Her face was cut and bruised, and Connie barely recognized her. She was deathly still. The rise and fall of the ventilator was the only noise in the room. Connie touched her hand and placed a small kiss on her pale cheek.

She left the room with Greg's arm supporting her. Outside, she leaned against the wall and waited for Dr. Hollis to come out with Mr. Sims. He told them, "Go home and get some rest. You can only see Erin in fifteen-minute increments while she's in Intensive Care. Once she's moved to a regular room, someone can stay with her." Connie didn't want to leave, but knew it made good sense.

She went outside into the cold morning air and waited for Greg to bring the car around. Mike Cook waited with her. He offered her his jacket when he noticed her shivering. She refused. The jacket wouldn't help. The cold she was feeling was not from the weather. She was afraid her friend was going to die. Her mind was too numb now for prayer, and fear had taken over her every thought.

Greg watched her expression as they approached the place where the accident had taken place. Connie's car had been pulled from the ravine and was sitting on the tow truck. He heard her gasp of dismay when she saw the condition of the car. He wondered if she was thinking the same thing that he'd thought when he first saw it.

She was. "Oh my God," she whispered. "How could she have survived that?" The front of the car was completely demolished. The hood had been pushed into the windshield, the driver's door was buckled, and the top of the car had caved. The rear of the vehicle wasn't much better shape. She felt Greg's hand cover hers, and she was comforted by his touch. Erin had survived. She needed to remember that. They passed by slowly. She could see where the car had left the road. Skid marks indicated that she'd slid several yards before plunging into the ravine. Connie brushed tears from her cheeks with the back of her hand.

Greg was glad when they were past the accident scene. Connie was so upset, and he hadn't wanted to come this way, but she had insisted. He wanted to get her home and tucked into bed as quickly as possible. He hadn't told her how close he'd been to driving away last night without finding Erin. He figured she didn't need to know that right now.

Back at the house, he waited on the front porch while she showered. He was planning to go by the accident scene once he left here. He was hoping she'd agree to lie down and rest. He could tell by the shadows under her eyes that she was exhausted.

The screen door opened, and she came out onto the porch. The shower hadn't erased the shadows from her eyes. She looked small and frail to him. He stood and put his arms around her. She rested her head against his chest and closed her eyes.

He held her like that for a few minutes, then led her back inside down the hallway and into her room. She didn't protest when he led her to the bed. She lay down, and he pulled the covers over her. Her eyes closed instantly, and her breathing deepened. He could tell that she was deeply asleep. He brushed the hair from her forehead with gentle fingers and placed a kiss on her rosy lips. She sighed in her sleep and rolled onto her side. He left the house, quietly locking the troublesome front door behind him.

Thirty-one

Back at the accident site, he joined Mike and they walked the road looking for anything that would give them a clue as to the cause of the crash. He and Mike were both troubled by the damage to the rear of the vehicle. An accident such as the one Erin had been in wouldn't account for that much damage to the rear of the car. They both suspected she'd been forced from the road. The only question in their mind was why. Only Erin would be able to explain what had happened, if she recovered from the coma.

They walked further up the road and they both spotted another set of skid marks. Bending down, Greg picked up some broken glass from the road. It might be from Connie's Mustang or from another vehicle. The lab would be able to tell him what he wanted to know. Returning to Mike's car, they drove slowly up and down the road looking for other evidence that another car had been involved.

Mike spotted the place where the grass was torn up alongside the road. Getting out, they scanned the area completely. It appeared as if someone had used the spot to turn quickly around. The grass was torn as if the car had been in a hurry. Greg called the station and asked for the forensics team to come and make plaster casts of the tire tracks. While they waited, he and Mike discussed the accident.

Looking at Greg, Mike chose his words carefully. "Have you considered the possibility that this might not have been meant for Erin? She was driving Connie's car, and it would have been too dark for anyone to be able to see who the driver was. I don't believe for one minute that this was an accident. Erin's driving record is clean. She drives this road all the time, and I don't think she would have been so careless."

Greg was somewhat surprised by the depth of feeling in Mike's words. He knew Mike found Erin attractive, but that he hadn't asked her out yet. Mike was quiet and shy. He found it hard to approach women. He dated infrequently and seldom dated the same woman more than twice. He'd once told Greg that it only took two dates for most women to realize that he was too quiet for their tastes. He'd laughed ruefully.

Greg had assured him that he'd find the right woman one day, never realizing at the time that he was dating the wrong woman himself. Irene Lawton had given him his walking papers shortly afterwards. Mike had been a good friend through the rough times. Greg looked up and spoke, "I've thought of little else since I realized that Erin was driving the Mustang. I almost didn't find her you know. If I hadn't skidded on that patch of ice, I'd have driven right by without ever knowing she was down there.

Mike looked up, surprised. "Maybe it was just an accident. You're an excellent driver. If you had trouble here then I guess it's reasonable to assume she might have also."

"I don't think so," Greg replied. "That wouldn't explain the damage to the rear of the car. No, someone forced her off the road. I'm sure of it."

"How did you know she was there?" Mike asked. "You surely couldn't see anything from up here."

"She blew the horn to signal for help. I almost drove away, though. She'd stopped blowing the horn, and I was about to leave. I thank God that she found the strength to signal again. I'd never have forgiven myself if she'd died down there. I plan to investigate this as if it was attempted murder. I'm sure it wasn't an accident. I don't want to worry Connie, so I'm not going to tell her what we suspect. She'll know soon enough if we're right."

Mike nodded in agreement. He had grown fond of Connie himself. She made Greg happy and that made her popular in his book.

The forensics team arrived, and Greg hastened to explain what he wanted done. "I want this area thoroughly searched. We're fairly certain this was no accident. I just need you guys to verify my suspicions."

They went to work at once, and Greg and Mike continued to look over the area. They didn't find anything else and left soon after. Mike returned to work, and Greg drove back to Connie's.

Connie had slept soundly for several hours and was feeling a bit more optimistic by the time Greg came back. She'd made some soup and sandwiches, which they shared sitting at the kitchen table.

They returned to the hospital around 2 p.m. There had been no change in Erin's condition. Her parents' faces were gray with fatigue. Connie offered to stay at the hospital for the rest of the day so that they could go home and rest. She agreed to call at once if there was any change. They accepted gratefully.

Greg stayed with Connie until five, and then left to go home and shower and change. He wanted to come back, but she told him not to. She knew he needed to work the next day, and she was concerned that he wouldn't get enough sleep. He ignored her and returned around eight.

Erin's parents came back soon after that. They had rested some and had rented a hotel room near the hospital before they returned. They didn't want to have to go so far from her bedside just to shower and change. Connie was glad to see them looking better. She knew how very worried they must be.

Erin was their youngest and only daughter. Her brother, Scott, lived in Tennessee and was away on a business trip to Alaska. He would be unable to come before the weekend. She hoped Erin would be better by then. She and Greg sat in the tiny waiting room in between visits to Erin's room. They prayed the Rosary several times during that long evening.

Around ten, she urged Greg to go home. He argued, but finally capitulated. He kissed her warmly and held her close for several minutes when she walked him down to the lobby. She returned to the waiting room and remained at the hospital for the rest of the night. She had asked for a substitute for the remainder of the week and was able to concentrate solely on Erin.

She visited the small chapel on the first floor of the hospital. It was a Catholic hospital, and the Blessed Sacrament was present in the tabernacle. She knelt there and prayed fervently. Tears were streaming down her cheeks when she finished. She sat for a time in the pew and composed herself.

She returned to the waiting room once more. Erin's parents were just coming from her room. She could tell by their faces that nothing had changed. Her own face must have mirrored her feelings as well. They hugged her and announced that they were going back to the hotel for a short while. Connie nodded and assured them that she would stay until morning.

She spent the rest of the long night reading from the bible she had brought from the chapel. Around 5 a.m., she looked in on Erin for the last time before leaving. She was still very pale and not breathing on her own. The doctor came in as she was leaving. He had no good news for her. She felt her eyes clouding again and hurriedly left the room.

In the bathroom, she splashed some water on her face and brushed her teeth with the toothbrush she always carried. Greg was coming at six to take her home, and she didn't want him to see what a mess she was. She ran a brush through her hair and straightened her clothes. *There,* she thought, *you look a little better anyway.*

Greg could see that Connie had had a rough night when she came down to the lobby. Her eyes were bright with unshed tears and though she tried to smile, he could see that it was an effort. He hugged her tightly and led her to the car. He took her straight home and fixed her some breakfast while she showered and changed. He watched as she picked at the food on her plate. "Hey," he said. "You need to eat. You've got to keep your strength up. You won't do Erin any good if you make yourself ill."

Connie nodded. "I know, but I don't have any appetite. Food is the last thing on my mind right now." She put some egg in her mouth and chewed. It tasted like sawdust. She swallowed with difficulty and took a long drink of the tea Greg had made. It scalded the roof of her mouth, and her eyes filled with tears. Greg jumped up and brought her a glass of cold milk. She sipped at it, and her mouth felt a little better. She ate a couple more bites of egg, and then pushed the plate across the table. Greg scraped the dishes and loaded them into the dishwasher.

He followed Connie to her room and watched as she slipped under the covers. He found himself wishing he could join her. Leaning over, he kissed her and she slipped her arms around his neck. She didn't want him to leave either.

He sat on the edge of the bed for a few minutes and held her hand. She watched him and knew this was the man she wanted to marry. She felt guilty at the happiness that filled her heart.

She had no right to be so happy when Erin was lying in the hospital near death. She prayed again for Erin and thanked God for her own happiness. She fell asleep smiling, holding tightly to Greg's hand.

Thirty-two

He sat for a long time watching her sleep. He had no doubt that God had intended this woman to be his. He had wanted everything to be perfect when he proposed, but he should have known life was never perfect. He wasn't going to waste anymore time. He kissed her gently and left her sleeping.

On his way to work, he made his plans. He was going to propose that evening. He would buy the ring this afternoon. It would have to be something special like Connie herself. He smiled as he imagined the look on her face when he popped the question. She would certainly be surprised. He never even considered the possibility that she might say no. He was sure she felt the same way he did.

He breezed through the day smiling. Mike kidded him about his perpetual smile, and he told him of his decision. Mike was supportive and enthusiastic.

It was 4:30 p.m., and he was about to leave work when Sheriff Fowler called him into his office. Adam Fowler was a good friend of Erin's father and had been following the investigation of Erin Sims' supposed accident very carefully. He trusted Greg's judgment and, after reading the lab report, was convinced that this had been no accident.

"Sit down," he said when Greg came into his office. "I've just gotten the lab report on those tire tracks and that broken glass you found near the scene of Erin's accident. The glass is from a front signal light on a late model Lincoln Towncar. The tire tracks match tires found on the same model, too. There's also evidence of silver gray paint taken from the bumper of the car she was driving that would fit that vehicle as well. This was no accident. Someone tried to kill that young woman. Got any ideas about this?"

Greg knew Sheriff Fowler was well aware of the ongoing investigation into the murder of Eleanor Lincoln. He always knew what was going on in his town. He answered carefully, "Mike and I both think that Connie was the intended victim. It was her car Erin was driving, and it was too dark for the identity of the driver to have been apparent. We are treating this as an attempted homicide. We're pretty sure it all ties in with Connie having seen the man suspected of the Lincoln homicide last Friday. I should have suspected something like this might happen. He must be getting desperate because he's starting to get careless."

Adam Fowler nodded thoughtfully. "Let me know if you need anything. I want this thing wrapped up pretty quickly. I'm going to assign your other cases to Deputy Crawford for the time being. I want you to concentrate solely on catching this monster."

Greg thanked him, assured him that he would keep him informed, and left the office. He knew he was going to have to tell Connie everything soon.

Later, at the jewelry store, he chose an antique diamond and sapphire ring. Set in gold, it had a half-carat diamond surrounded by smaller sapphires. The gold band was etched with intricate filigree in the shape of tiny roses. He knew immediately it was the perfect ring for Connie. She always smelled slightly of roses. He bought the ring and left.

He called Connie at home, but got her machine. She had probably gone back to the hospital. He decided not to call her cell phone because she was required to turn it off while she was there. He would just go straight to the hospital. Perhaps she would go to dinner with him. If not, he would follow her home and propose there. He was still smiling when he arrived at the hospital.

She wasn't in the waiting room or in Erin's room. Erin's mother suggested he try the chapel. He walked quickly down the hall to the elevator.

Back on the first floor, he followed the signs to the chapel. He found her there praying in front of the statue of Mary. He was hesitant to disturb her and was backing away when she looked up. She motioned to him, and he joined her there. At the feet of the Blessed Virgin, they prayed together.

Connie had returned to the hospital around 3 p.m. She stayed with Erin's parents in the waiting room, and they prayed the Rosary together. She decided to go back to the chapel at 5:30. She knew at once when Greg was there. She was glad then he joined her to pray.

When they were done, they genuflected before the tabernacle and exited quietly. In the hall, Greg placed a quick kiss on her lips and slipped his arm around her shoulders. They walked slowly back to the elevator and went upstairs.

They talked with Erin's parents and visited her room twice more. Dr. Hollis came in as they were about to leave. He seemed a bit more optimistic today as he talked to them. "The nurses have noticed some slight movement of Erin's hand, and her pupils have reacted to bright light. It could still be days before we know anything definite, but these are positive signs."

Erin's mother sagged against her husband and wept with joy. Connie, too, shed tears at the good news. They left the hospital, and Greg suggested getting dinner. She agreed, and they decided to eat at Mario's. She looked up in surprise when Greg ordered a bottle of champagne. "Are we celebrating something?" she asked.

"Sure," he said with a smile. "We're celebrating Erin's improving health."

"I guess that's a great reason to celebrate. I just hope we're not being premature," she responded.

"Come on honey, let's be positive," he said firmly. "No sad thoughts tonight." He reached across the table and took her hand. Lifting it, he brushed his lips softly across the back. Connie blushed when she saw the passion flare in his eyes. She removed her hand and put it in her lap.

The waiter brought the champagne and poured it into two crystal flutes. They toasted Erin's continued improvement. During dinner, they drank tea and saved the remainder of the champagne for later. They danced for a time on the small floor, and then he led her back to the table. They declined dessert and sat talking quietly.

Greg refilled the champagne glasses and once more took her by the hand. Looking into her eyes he said, "Connie, will you marry me?"

Her eyes filled with tears of joy as she whispered her answer, "Yes."

Greg took the ring from his pocket and slipped it onto her finger. She gasped at the beauty of it. "Oh, Greg! This is the most beautiful ring I've ever seen!"

The ring was a perfect fit, and he was delighted with her response to it. He came around the table and led her back to the dance floor. They danced slowly, savoring the moment.

At the table once more, they made some plans for their life together. They both wanted a small wedding with family and friends at the Catholic church. They decided to discuss which church later. They both wanted to start a family soon, and Connie said, "I want to stay at home and raise our children." Greg agreed with her wholeheartedly.

They put off choosing a date for the ceremony. Greg wanted to speak to his parents first, and Connie knew they would need to consult with Father Murphy as well. Also, they agreed to wait as long as necessary for Erin to be able to attend. Greg was happier than he'd thought possible. Looking at her, he could see the glow he was feeling mirrored in her eyes. He decided not to spoil her happiness with the information he had learned that afternoon. Tomorrow would be soon enough.

He followed her home and checked the house thoroughly before he left. She stood at the window, waving until she could no longer see his car. She took a long hot bath and, sitting in bed, sorted through the mail that had accumulated these last several days. She was glad tomorrow was Saturday. She would visit Erin and then go shopping for a new dress. Greg was taking her back to his parents' house on Sunday, and she wanted something special to wear. She said her Rosary and then fell asleep with her left hand cradling her cheek.

Thirty-three

He scanned the front page looking for the story on the accident. It had been two days now, and surely it would be front-page news in this one-horse town. People didn't die in car crashes very often in Rosemount.

The story was on page five. Reading it, he felt his blood pressure soaring. It had all been for nothing. Someone else had been driving her car. Furious, he continued reading. The Sims woman was listed as being in a coma and not expected to recover. *Well, at least she won't be able to tell anyone that she was forced off the road,* he thought.

There was no mention of the owner of the car, and the sheriff apparently was treating this as just another accident on an icy road. He smiled when he finished reading the story. There would be other chances to get to her. He knew where she worked, where she shopped, where she lived. There was still time.

He stood up and stretched, looking slowly around the living room. This place was a mess. His wife still hadn't come home, and he had no interest in cleaning up after himself. That was her job.

He went into the garage and looked at the car. He'd better take it to the body shop this afternoon. The front light was broken, and there was a scratch on the front fender. He planned to tell them that he'd slid on a patch of ice and hit a tree. With what they would charge to fix the thing, they wouldn't care what he'd done. They would only be interested in future repair jobs.

He went back inside and decided to call his sister-in-law. Maybe she'd know where his wife was. She was polite, but denied knowing anything. He slammed the phone down hard. Her husband needed to show her what a real man was. That simpering wimp let her lead him around like a donkey. She wouldn't treat him like that if he were her husband. He tried his in-laws as well, but they didn't answer.

He went through the pile of mail lying on the hall table. Most of it was junk, but the large manila envelope at the bottom of the pile was different. The return address made him break into a cold sweat. James Reed, Attorney at Law.

He knew without opening it what it contained. His rage boiled. He smashed the mirror over the console in the hall with his fist. Cursing, he tore open the envelope. She had filed for divorce. He hadn't thought she had it in her. His heart sank when he read the terms. She'd apparently been to see the accountant. She was planning to leave him with nothing.

Going to the phone, he called the bank. They informed him that his wife had closed their joint accounts on the previous afternoon. They were solicitous, but could offer no help. He hung up cursing. She'd rue the day she crossed him, he promised himself. For now, though, he'd have to take care of his other problem. Thrusting the papers in the console drawer, he went upstairs to shower.

He took the car to the body shop and left it. They promised it would be ready in just a few days. The loaner car was another Lincoln. He drove slowly back to town. He went to the school where Connie worked. He pretended to be the parent of one of her students. The school secretary told him that she would be out for the remainder of the week.

He left the school wondering what to do next. He decided to visit a sick friend at the hospital. She was likely there visiting her friend, the Sims woman. They must be close friends. She'd been driving her car Wednesday night. He entered the hospital through the side door. He didn't want to chance meeting the cop she was dating.

He asked the young volunteer at the desk for Ms. Sims room number. She blushed as he stared at her breasts and stammered the room number. He winked and thanked her for the information.

He took the back elevator and almost bumped into Connie as she came from the room. He ducked into a nearby supply room and listened through a crack in the door as she left. He waited for about five minutes, then slipped into the Intensive Care Unit.

Erin Sims lay in the bed not moving. There were so many tubes running to and from her body that he couldn't even count them all. He slipped back out the door. She was no threat to him.

He left the hospital through the same side door and drove slowly through the parking lot looking for Connie. She was nowhere in sight. He gave up when he saw the security guard looking at him suspiciously. He returned home and lay down to take a nap. Later, after dark, he would try once more to find his prey.

Thirty-four

Connie awakened with a start when the sirens blared on the road outside. Her heart was pounding with fright as she hurried to the window. Looking out, she saw the squad car sitting in her driveway with its lights flashing. She hurried to the front door just as the pounding and shouting began.

Mike was about to bash the door in when he heard Connie working the lock. She assured him she was fine and opened the door. She had recognized his voice when he called to her and hadn't hesitated to open the door. "What's going on?" she queried in a shaky voice as he came through the door.

Mike looked quickly around the house before answering her, "A neighbor saw a prowler outside your window and called the sheriff's office. He was gone by the time I arrived, though." He knew that Greg had not told her of their suspicions yet. Well, he was going to have to tell her now. She needed to know.

Connie had stopped shaking, but was still feeling a bit unnerved. She wondered about the prowler. She'd never had any problems in the past with such things. Suddenly she gasped, and her hand flew to cover her mouth. *What if it had been Eleanor's killer prowling about the house?*

Mike caught her by the arm as she swayed and led her to the couch. He'd noticed the ring when she covered her mouth. He knew now why Greg hadn't told her last night. He'd been too busy proposing marriage.

He wasn't going to tell her that he'd been watching her house all night long. He had been the one to see the man crouching outside her bedroom window. Greg could tell her everything later. It wasn't his job, and he was glad. He was only sorry he hadn't caught the prowler.

He hadn't wanted to follow him into the woods and leave Connie unprotected. They really needed more than one man to do the job properly. He'd called for backup, but it had been too late in coming. The man was long gone now. In the morning, they would search the grounds for clues. For now, though, he would stay here. Greg could be told tomorrow. There was nothing he could do until then anyway. He'd be mad, but he'd get over it.

"Are you okay?" he asked Connie. She nodded hesitantly and gladly agreed that he could spend the rest of his shift on her couch. It was 3 a.m., and she knew she'd never be able to get back to sleep.

She made coffee and shared it with Mike. They talked, and she asked him about himself. She was easy to talk to, and he found himself telling her things that he'd never told another woman.

She listened attentively and was happy to be thinking about something other than the prowler. Mike kept mentioning Erin, and she decided that as soon as Erin was well she would set them up. Erin would like him. He would be the perfect opposite for her. He was quiet and shy. Well-spoken without being pompous, good looking in a quiet way, and he had plans for his life. He wasn't Catholic, but Erin could work on that.

Mike called Greg around eight. He was angry. He started shouting as soon as he heard what had happened. Mike put Connie on the phone, and she was able to calm him somewhat. She assured him she was fine and urged him not to rush over to the house. He ignored her, and thirty minutes later was standing on her front porch. He gave Mike a baleful look, but Mike merely grinned and returned to his perusal of the morning paper.

Connie fixed Greg a cup of coffee, and he and Mike sat in the kitchen while she fixed breakfast. Over scrambled eggs and sausage, Mike suggested that Greg tell her what was really going on with the case. Connie looked at Greg in confusion. "What does he mean?" she asked.

Greg glared at Mike again, but he knew it was time. "Mike and I think that someone tried to kill Erin," he said bluntly. Mike winced at the way Connie paled. *Greg could certainly use some practice breaking bad news*, he thought. Greg's next words confirmed that thought. "We think they meant to kill you. It was just bad timing that Erin was driving your car. We're pretty sure it had something to do with the Lincoln case."

"Oh no," she gasped.

Greg put his arm around her shoulders and hugged her close. He believed in getting right to the point, but he wished he'd been able to soften the blow a bit.

Connie struggled to understand how someone could have deliberately tried to kill Erin. *No*, she thought, *it wasn't Erin they wanted to kill. It was me.* She pulled away from Greg and stood.

She paced the kitchen floor trying to regain control of her rampaging thoughts. She was picturing Erin lying in that hospital bed, tubes controlling her every bodily function. What if Erin died? How would she be able to live with the guilt she would feel knowing that she had been the intended victim? *Erin is not going to die,* she told herself firmly. *Remember, her condition is improving. Doctor Hollis had said so.* She took a deep breath and turned to the two men at the table. "Tell me what I can do to help," she said firmly.

"There's nothing you can do at the moment," Greg responded. "Go and visit Erin, and Mike and I will continue our investigation. We're going to bring some other deputies out today to search for anything our prowler might have left. I'll drive you to the hospital and come back for you later."

"No. I'm not going to let this maniac rule my life anymore. It's broad daylight now, and I can't imagine he'll try anything more today." She was adamant, and Greg finally gave into her. She agreed to call when she got to the hospital and when she left. She told him she was going shopping later and refused to change her plans. He didn't like it, but she wouldn't budge. She left the kitchen to shower and change.

In the shower, Connie tried to recapture some of the magic of the previous evening. She failed. Even the ring on her finger couldn't bring a smile. She dressed in jeans, a pink sweater, and a matching denim jacket. She applied rose eye shadow, blush, and a soft rose lipstick. She brushed her hair and pulled a heavy jacket from her closet. She left her room and returned to the kitchen.

The men had cleared the table and loaded the dishwasher. She could hear them talking, outside on the porch. On her way out, she kissed Greg and drove away in the pickup. She needed to call the insurance company about her car. The agent had called on Friday, when she was at the hospital. Her car had been totaled. She needed to go car shopping as well.

At the hospital, she met Erin's parents and her older brother in the lobby. Scott was tall and good-looking like Erin. He had deep green eyes and dark blonde hair. He had always teased

Connie unmercifully when they were kids, and she loved him as much as she did Erin. He'd married his high school sweetheart and moved away eight years ago. He had four children now and was vice president of the bank where he worked.

He hugged Connie tightly and said, "You look great! Why hasn't some man had the good sense to carry you off yet?" Connie laughed, but hid her ring hand behind her back. She didn't want to flaunt her happiness while Erin was so sick.

Upstairs, Dr. Hollis was waiting for them. He was smiling, and Connie's heart lifted. He must have good news. He did. "Erin regained consciousness an hour ago. She remembers everything that happened and is breathing on her own now. She's asleep at the moment, but as soon as she wakes up, you can all see her." They sat talking excitedly while they waited.

An hour later, they were ushered into the room. Erin's eyes were open, and she was muttering under her breath as they came near her. She stopped when she saw them and reached out to her mom and dad. They hugged her tightly, and Connie and Scott stood back near the door. A minute later they, too, were hugging her. Connie started crying, and Erin said, "Hey, I know I look bad, but not that bad."

Connie wiped her eyes and laughed shakily. "You've never looked more beautiful to me," she said fondly. Erin was acting like her old self. It was as if she had never been in a coma. When the nurse came in, she asked when she could get some real food.

The nurse offered to bring her some broth, and Erin snorted derisively. "I was thinking more along the lines of steak and potatoes," she said. The nurse laughed and promised to see what she could do. When she left, Erin asked, "Did they find that jerk that ran me off the road yet? I think he meant to kill me."

Connie exchanged looks with Erin's parents before she answered.

Mr. Sims glanced at his wife before nodding to Connie. Sheriff Fowler had discussed his suspensions with him and his wife, but they had not had the opportunity to speak with Connie.

"The sheriff thinks that I was the intended victim, not you," she said. "I'm so sorry, Erin. If I hadn't let you use the car, you wouldn't be hurt." Her eyes filled with tears once more.

"Well next time just tell me no," Erin teased.

Connie smiled a little at that and reached for Erin's hand. It was then that Erin spotted the ring on her left hand. "When did that happen?" she squealed. "Have you been holding out on me these last few weeks?"

"It happened last night if you must know," Connie replied. "So I could hardly be holding out on you."

"When's the wedding?" Erin asked. "Will I have time to grow some new hair? I'd hate to be the maid of honor with this big bald spot on my head."

Laughing, Connie assured her that it would be at least four months before the wedding.

"I would have waited longer if need be for you to get well. I'd never have considered letting anyone else be my maid of honor."

"Well, I should hope not," Erin, retorted. "After all, I am your best friend."

They stayed until the nurse returned and shooed them out of the room. "You can come back in a couple of hours if you like," she said. "Right now, my patient needs rest." Erin made a face, and they were laughing as they left the room. They didn't notice the tall man lingering in the hallway.

Thirty-five

He watched them leaving and wondered at their apparent happiness. When he saw the nurse leave, he approached the door. He opened it slowly and looked into the room. She didn't look any different to him. He closed the door and left the hospital.

In the parking lot, he spotted Connie again. She was chatting with the tall man who had come out of the room with her. He wondered what had happened to the cop. *Probably still hanging around her house,* he thought.

He'd been ready to go in through the window last night when the cop car pulled in with lights on and sirens blaring. Scared, he'd run quickly into the woods. He'd hiked back to his car and quickly left. No one seemed to remember that old gravel road that he'd used so often this last month. He was sure no one knew who he was yet or what he was up to. He was a very clever man.

He watched Connie as she hugged the tall man and then climbed into the pickup. He walked quickly to his car and followed her as she left the parking lot. He was grateful for the tinted windows that made it hard to see into his car. He stayed several cars behind when she pulled onto Main Street.

He parked across the street when she pulled into the spot in front of a small boutique. He was about to leave his car when the squad car pulled into a nearby spot in the same lot. He recognized the tall deputy at the wheel. He pretended to be reading the paper and was relieved when the deputy passed by without even glancing his way.

Thirty-six

Greg crossed the street and entered Rachel's. He spotted Connie at the rear of the store, talking with the salesperson. She looked up in surprise when he appeared at her elbow. He thought she looked a little irritated. He was right.

"What are you doing here?" she asked somewhat querulously. She realized that she had neglected to call as she had promised when she left the hospital.

"I was looking for you. I called the hospital, and the nurse said you'd left. You promised you'd let me know where you were going to be," he answered defensively.

"I didn't think I would be in any danger here," she said. "I just wanted to shop for a little while. This is the only store I was planning to go to. I've known Rachel for years, and I knew she'd have what I was looking for today."

"I'm sorry, honey. I was worried when I couldn't reach you at the hospital. I just happened to spot you as I was on my way to the station. Forgive me?" he asked with a winsome smile.

Connie was hard-pressed to resist that smile or the look in his eyes. Reaching up, she kissed him and then introduced him to the woman who had been watching the interchange with amusement.

Rachel Pierce had been a school friend, and they had stayed in touch since graduation. She hadn't married either, but was a successful businesswoman. Her boutique carried one-of-a-kind dresses, suits, and feminine accessories. She was tall, slim, and tanned. Her brilliant green eyes sparkled with fun as she shook Greg's hand. "I promise I'll take good care of Connie if you'd like to wait outside for her," she said.

"I'll leave her in your capable hands then," Greg responded. He went outside and sank onto a bench. He watched the people passing by on the street as he waited for Connie to emerge.

With Rachel's help, Connie chose several outfits to try. She decided on two of them. One was a long, straight, emerald-green skirt with a matching cowl-necked sweater. The other was the dress she planned to wear the following day to her future in-laws.

The color was a deep ruby red. The sweetheart neckline emphasized her small shoulders and her slender neck. The bodice was tightly fitted, but the skirt was full and swirled softly around her ankles. She had never felt more feminine in her life. She was sure Greg would love it, too.

She purchased a pair of shoes and a handbag with a peacock-feather design to go with the dress. She left the store with a smile on her face. Today was turning out to be a wonderful day.

Greg watched her emerge from the store, and he was delighted by the joy he could see in her face. Standing up, he kissed her and offered to take her to eat. They had lunch at a deli across the street.

Over lunch, she told him of Erin's progress and wished she'd remembered to call him from the hospital. He looked a little hurt that she'd neglected to share something that important with him. "I'm sorry I forgot to call. I was so excited by it all, and Scott and I hadn't seen each other for years that I just forgot."

"Who's Scott?" Greg asked nonchalantly. He was feeling anything but. He'd seen the way her face lit up when she said his name. The green-eyed monster had taken possession of him.

Noticing the look on his face, she decided to tease him a little. "Scott is Erin's older brother. I had quite a crush on him when we were teenagers," she said. "He told me today that if he'd known how great I was going to turn out, he would have hung around more."

The green-eyed monster roared in Greg's ear, and he spoke, "So just how long is Scott going to be in town?"

Connie was sorry now that she'd teased him. "Scott will be going back to Tennessee tomorrow. He'll be back for Christmas, though, with his wife Rebecca and their four kids. I can't wait to see Rebecca again. It's been eight years since they moved away."

Greg was relieved to learn that Scott was married. He relaxed again and told her what he and Mike had learned that morning. They had followed the trail through the woods to the old gravel road that ran along CR 358. They had found tire tracks there and footprints that probably belonged to the prowler. There was no doubt in Greg's mind that this was the same man that had murdered Eleanor Lincoln.

He informed Connie that she would have round-the-clock police protection until he was caught. That was why he'd been so concerned when he'd been told she'd left the hospital without letting anyone know where she was going.

Connie sighed heavily, her happiness once again overshadowed by the monster in her life. She wondered how much longer it would be before he made another mistake and would be caught.

Greg watched the shadows fill her eyes and was saddened. The joy of their engagement had been so fleeting. He prayed to God that it would return soon. He hated to see the love of his life so unhappy. Cupping her cheek with his fingers, he lifted her face to his and said, "I promise you I'm going to catch this guy before he hurts anyone else."

"I know you will," she said. Her faith in Greg had never been in question. It was her faith in human nature that sometimes faltered.

They left the deli and returned to the hospital. Erin was again sleeping, and they chose not to disturb her. Greg followed Connie home, and they spent the afternoon together. They took a long walk, in the cold afternoon air, and returned to the house to spend the remainder of the day by the fire.

Connie prepared a light supper and once again made the bed in the spare room for Greg. *This is getting to be a habit*, she thought. Her thoughts wandered into the future, as she envisioned what their life would be like once they were married. She was standing by the bed holding a pillow, smiling slightly, when Greg walked into the room.

He wondered what she was thinking about. At least they appeared to be happy thoughts. He was relieved to see the smile on her face once more. It had been a difficult time for her lately. He knew she was still feeling guilty about the accident, but Erin's return to consciousness seemed to have raised her spirits tremendously.

She looked up and saw him standing there. She smiled and accepted his help with the bed sheets. When they were done, she kissed him goodnight and went to her room. She prepared for bed and then said her Rosary. She prayed for strength. Her resolve was weak when Greg was there at night. Four months seemed like forever. Thank goodness he seemed to have an iron will.

Greg was praying for the same thing in his room. His iron will was faltering, but he was determined to do the right thing. He lay in bed and prayed the Rosary also. Since meeting Connie, he was certainly praying a lot more. He supposed that two good things had come out of this tragedy.

Thirty-seven

When the deputy went inside the boutique, he left. He was starting to get a little nervous. The cops seemed to be everywhere he went these days. He was going to have to end this thing soon. He returned home to find that nothing had changed. He looked over the divorce papers again and was once more enraged. There would be no divorce!

He would see to that. He wasn't going to kowtow to her after all these years. He tore the papers in half and left them strewn on the living room floor. He went out for a bite to eat.

He drove into Charlotte and went to one of the clubs he had frequented in the past. He made small talk with the bartender while he ate a sandwich. He surveyed the dance floor looking for someone to spend time with this evening.

The tall blonde sitting alone at a corner table caught his eye, and he sauntered over to her. She smiled when he offered to buy her a drink and invited him to sit down. An hour later, she invited him to come home with her. *Women are so easy*, he thought. Ply them with compliments and a few drinks and they'll do whatever you want. He laughed to himself as he followed her out of the club.

Thirty-eight

There was frost on the ground when Connie looked out the window Sunday morning. She could hear the shower going in the hall bathroom and knew Greg was already up. She showered and dressed for church.

The new dress fit perfectly, and she felt beautiful in it. She applied her makeup with extra care and added mascara to her already long eyelashes. She slipped into the pumps and filled the new purse. One last glance in the mirror, then she left her room.

Greg was sitting on the couch when she walked into the living room. He stood up, and she could see the admiration in his eyes when he saw her. "You look so beautiful," he said as he put his arms around her. She blushed at the look in his eyes, but didn't pull away from him. He kissed her softly and held her close for several moments.

Greg pulled back and looked down at Connie. Her lips and cheeks were rosy, and he could see the love in her eyes. He helped her with her coat, and they left for church. It felt wonderful to be with her at Mass. She made him feel complete. He could barely remember his life without her. He knew it had been lonely, though.

After Mass, they met with Father Murphy and asked him to post the banns for their marriage. He reminded them of the classes they must attend, and Connie agreed to call on Monday to get the schedule. Greg took her to breakfast, and then they went to his parents' house.

Greg's parents greeted them warmly, and his mother slipped her arm through Connie's as they walked into the living room. They sat in the large living room, and Greg told his parents about the engagement. In his usual forthright way he said, "Connie and I are getting married."

Carol Reed's eyes filled with tears as she hugged her son. When she turned to Connie, she said simply, "Welcome to our family, dear."

Connie's eyes filled with tears, too, at the warm sentiment. She had been afraid they would think it was too soon. James Reed hugged her and welcomed her as well.

Greg's brothers and his sister Patricia showed up around two for dinner with their families. Connie was disappointed when she heard Carol say to the others, "Carron won't be joining us today. She's busy packing. She's going to visit her friend Kathryn in Florida for a few days. Connie noticed Greg's mouth tighten at the news, and she wondered if marital troubles were the reason Carron was leaving. She slipped her hand into his, and the smile returned to his face.

They enjoyed a wonderful dinner of roast beef, mashed potatoes, green beans, and homemade bread. They sat around the dinner table talking and laughing. After dinner, Greg's father raised his glass and toasted Greg and Connie. The others offered their congratulations and Patricia asked, "Have you set the date?"

Greg replied, "We're planning for mid-June." No one seemed surprised that they didn't want to wait too long.

Carol said, "You had better get busy planning, or you'll never pull it off that quickly."

She offered Connie her help, as did Patricia and Greg's sisters-in-law. They all looked excited at the prospect of a wedding. They talked of little else until they left around six.

Connie and Greg stopped at the hospital to visit Erin before going home. She had been moved into a private room and was watching TV when they arrived. She was feeling much better, but still looked the worse for wear. Her head was bandaged, and the bruises on her face were still vivid. Her IV line had been removed, though, and she was able to move around a little. She complained about the food and said she was ready to go home.

Dr. Hollis came while they were there and assured Erin, "You'll be up and around in no time." He left without giving her a definite discharge date, much to her disgust. Connie and Greg stayed for about an hour and then went home.

It was almost 9 p.m. now, and it was bitterly cold outside. Connie turned the heat up and went to work in her office for a bit. She needed to make some changes to her lesson plans for the coming week. She realized she was too tired almost immediately. Her eyes kept closing, and her thoughts wandered. She gave up after fifteen minutes and went back to the living room where Greg was sitting reading. She sat beside him and leaned her head on his shoulder. She fell asleep within minutes.

Greg watched her sleep, then lifted her into his arms and carried her to bed. She nestled close in his arms, and he was loath to put her down. He stood for a minute beside the bed, holding her close before lowering her gently. He pulled the covers over her and kissed her softly before turning to leave.

175

At the door, he looked back at her. She was sleeping peacefully, her hand resting under her cheek. He left the room and prepared for bed. He prayed tonight for help in solving the case and for Connie's continued safety.

Thirty-nine

On her way to work Monday morning, Connie realized she was glad it was almost time for Christmas break. One more week after this one and she would have a two-week break. She was really looking forward to that. She had always loved Christmas and was looking forward to sharing it with Greg and his family. Things would be so different this year. She was part of a family again, and she liked the feeling.

The day passed uneventfully, and she was home by 4:30. Her police escort for the day was Mike. She invited him in for some coffee, and he accepted gratefully. It got cold sitting out in the car this time of year. Besides, he relished the opportunity to talk with Connie about Erin. He'd gone by to see her yesterday, but she'd been sleeping. He'd left without waking her.

He drank the coffee Connie fixed, and they chatted. He was shy about asking too many questions about Erin, but he didn't have to be. Connie seemed to know what he wanted to hear and talked at great length about her friend.

She reached over and touched his hand. He looked up startled, and she said. "Erin is a great person and a wonderful friend. I think she'd love to see you. Why don't we go back up to the hospital together? I'd like to see her myself and, after all, you have to go wherever I go."

Mike nodded enthusiastically, and they drove to the hospital together. He called Greg from the car to let him know where they were going. Greg was working the late shift today and wouldn't be off till 11 p.m. He would be coming by Connie's house then.

Erin was happy to see both her visitors. Her parents had just left, and she hadn't been looking forward to an evening of television. She wondered about Mike's presence, and then assumed he was watching out for Connie. Her parents had told her that Sheriff Fowler had ordered round-the-clock protection, and she was glad.

She studied Mike as he stood hesitantly by the door. He was good-looking in a quiet way. He was tall with wavy, black hair, dark eyes, and an olive complexion. He must have felt her stare because he looked up suddenly. She blushed at the intent look he gave her. She quickly looked away from him.

She concentrated on Connie, and they talked about the wedding until it was time to leave. Before he left, Mike came near the bed. "I'm glad you're doing so much better. I was concerned about you. I came by yesterday, but you were sleeping."

Erin blushed again at the thought of him watching her while she slept. Looking at him, she said softly, "Thank you for coming by. I appreciate your kindness." She wanted to say more, but didn't know what. She looked away again, confused. She'd never had this trouble before with men. The glib remarks she'd always made seemed wrong for this man. He turned away and left.

Watching her friend, Connie was amazed. *What had happened to the loquacious Erin she'd always known?* She seemed to be having trouble stringing two sentences together today. *Could it be that Mike was the cause? Who would have thought it?* She hugged Erin and whispered mischievously "What's the matter? You're usually much more coherent. Is it the head injury, or Mike, that has you confused?"

Erin glared back and then smiled. "You know I'm always in awe of our city's finest," she quipped. They laughed, and then Connie walked out into the hallway.

Mike was leaning against the wall, but straightened up when he saw her. *He looks a bit dazed,* she thought. Erin had been having that effect on men all of her adult life. Connie found it amazing that Erin seemed to be suffering the same malady herself. That was a first!

Mike was quiet as he walked with Connie to the car. He was thinking about Erin. Even with the bruises and bandages, she was the most beautiful woman he'd ever seen. He wished he found it easier to talk to her, though. He was sure she was used to more exciting men.

Mike wondered why he found it so much easier to talk with Connie than with Erin. He shrugged mentally. Maybe it would get easier with time. He fully intended to see Erin as often as possible. It was funny, though. Everything he'd heard about her seemed to indicate that she was very outgoing. She'd seemed almost shy tonight. They were at the car now, and he held the door for Connie. She was quiet as well, and the trip home passed in silence.

He noticed the front door was sticking when Connie tried to open it. He shoved hard against it, and it swung open. He checked inside the house, then had Connie lock the door while he looked around outside. Everything appeared normal, and he returned to the house. Again, he had to shove hard to get the door open. It was almost as difficult to close.

Connie fixed some sandwiches for the two of them, and they watched TV while they ate. They were both wrapped up in their own thoughts. It was almost ten o'clock when Connie announced she was going to prepare for bed. Mike nodded and watched as she left the room.

Connie was dismayed to realize that she was too tired to wait up for Greg. She brushed her teeth, washed her face, and then put on her nightgown. She climbed under the covers and said her evening prayers. She tried to stay awake, but couldn't.

She dreamed of the murderer again, only this time she was able to see his face. He was smiling at her, but it wasn't a pleasant smile. It was sinister, evil. She could see the evil in his cold eyes as well. She turned to go, but he reached for her hand and pulled her close. She could feel his cold breath on her face as he lowered his head to kiss her. Frightened and trembling, she tried to pull away from him. Holding her tightly, he began to speak.

His voice was harsh, and the words he uttered were ugly. He laughed as he told her about Eleanor's death and about Erin's, too. She knew Erin wasn't dead, but she didn't tell him. She was quiet as he told her of her own impending death.

He laughed at her puny struggles as she tried to push him away from her. She began calling for Greg and that made him angry. He pulled a shiny knife from his belt and began rubbing it across her throat. She was screaming, and he was laughing maniacally. Fear tightened her throat, and she was barely able to scream now. He looked pleased by that, and she knew it would be over soon. She began sobbing and pleading with him. He merely shook his head and smiled his cold smile as he raised the knife once more.

Greg arrived around 11:30 and sent Mike home. He looked in on Connie, but since she was sleeping he didn't disturb her. He lay down in the other room and was soon dozing.

He was awakened a short time later by sounds of sobbing emanating from Connie's room. He threw on a robe and hurried to her room. She was sobbing in her sleep. Tears were streaming down her face, and she appeared to be struggling to get from under the covers.

He turned the bedside lamp on and pulled the covers down to her waist. She was still sobbing so he shook her carefully, trying to wake her without startling her too much. She didn't respond, so he began whispering her name.

The sound of Greg's voice whispering her name drew Connie from the web of the nightmare. She awoke slowly, and it took a minute for her to orient herself. Greg was stroking her hair tenderly and whispering sweet words of love.

Sitting up, she nestled into his arms and he held her close. They stayed that way for a long time, happy to be together. Finally, Connie leaned back against her pillows. Greg was watching her anxiously, and she reached up to stroke the lines of worry from his forehead.

"It was just a bad dream," she said. "I was fighting with him and couldn't get away."

Greg didn't need to ask whom she'd been fighting with in her dream. "I heard you crying and tried to wake you up. I couldn't get you to open your eyes until I started calling to you."

"It was your voice that brought me out," Connie said. "It was so different from his. I knew you would help me if I could only open my eyes."

"I'm glad I was here. I don't want you to be scared. I'm going to take care of you," Greg said. "I'm going to spend the rest of the night in the chair. I want to be near if you need me again."

"I'll be fine now that I know you're here. Go back to bed. You need to get some rest. I know you have to work again tomorrow," Connie said.

"I'm staying right here. I've slept in worse places than a soft chair before. I'll just prop my feet on the end of the bed, and I'll be plenty comfortable," he assured her.

Greg leaned over and kissed her. Standing up, he pulled the wing-backed chair nearer the bed and sat down. He stretched his long legs out onto the foot of the bed and closed his eyes.

Feeling safe now, Connie slipped back to sleep. Greg opened his eyes when he heard her deep, even breathing. He watched her sleeping, and his eyelids soon became heavy. True to his word, he slept. Neither he nor Connie awakened again until morning.

She was the first to awaken around six. She stretched and was surprised when her foot touched something at the bottom of the bed. When she saw Greg sleeping in the chair, it all came flooding back. The nightmare, Greg's comforting presence, and his insistence on staying with her. She wondered for the hundredth time what she had done to be worthy of such love. Whatever it was, she was going to be thankful and enjoy every minute of it.

She slipped from bed quietly, careful not to awaken him, and went into the bathroom. She showered quickly and, wearing her robe, she went back into the bedroom. Greg was still sleeping as she stole softly by and went to the kitchen. She put some coffee on and decided to make breakfast.

The smell of brewing coffee and frying bacon brought Greg into the day. He yawned hugely and was surprised to find that it was after six. He walked down the hallway and into the kitchen. Connie was standing at the stove.

The morning sun coming in through the kitchen windows gave her an ethereal beauty. She was fresh and rosy from her shower and, coming up behind her, he slipped his arms around her.

She leaned back against his chest and tilted her head back to look into his eyes. He leaned down and kissed her. Turning in his arms, she twined her arms around his neck. She was kissing him now; warm, passionate kisses that spoke of the love she was feeling. A bit bemused, Greg looked down at her. She smiled sweetly and turned back to the stove.

"Breakfast will be ready in just a few minutes. You have time for a quick shower if you'd like. Would you like your eggs scrambled or sunny side up?" she asked.

"Sunny side up will be fine," he mumbled still reeling from the effects of her kiss. He left the kitchen and was soon standing under the spray of the shower. He brushed his teeth, shaved, and dressed quickly. She was just putting the eggs on his plate when he returned to the kitchen.

"Sit down," she said with a gentle smile. She poured steaming coffee into his cup and then took her own seat at the table. She offered grace and they ate, enjoying the morning. They cleared the table and by 7:15, left for work. Greg dropped her off at school and went on to the police station.

The day passed quickly for both of them, and they went to the hospital at 5 p.m. to visit Erin. She was ecstatic. "Dr. Hollis says that I can go home on Friday," she said happily. "I can't wait to get out of here!"

Connie and Greg laughed as they listened to her. She was planning on making up for lost time. She fully intended to do everything she'd missed the previous weekend. She was muttering about hospital food again when the door opened slowly and Mike stepped into the room.

Connie was again amazed at the change in Erin's demeanor. She was once again quiet and almost shy in his presence. For once, though, Mike didn't seem to be having any trouble. Apparently he, too, was planning to make up for lost time.

Greg listened in astonishment as Mike asked, "Would you like to have dinner with me Saturday, Erin?" Erin's answer was a quiet yes, and Mike was grinning. Then he appeared to remember that Connie and Greg were in the room. He was a little embarrassed, but soon got over it.

They laughed and talked for another thirty minutes, and then Greg and Connie began to leave. Mike was still sitting by the bed talking with Erin as they left. Greg looked at Connie and smiled. He wanted Mike to be as happy as he was. Feeling exuberant, he swung Connie around and kissed her soundly. She grinned. She was as happy as he was. They held hands as they walked to the parking lot.

Back at home, Deputy Crawford took over the watch, but Greg still spent the night in the spare room. He had decided to stay as close as possible until this thing was finished.

Forty

Wednesday brought colder temperatures and cloudy gray skies. Connie awakened happy, though, and went through the day smiling. Greg was busy following some leads in the Lincoln case during the time Connie was at school, so another deputy stayed with her.

At lunchtime, Greg received a call from his mother. "Can you and Connie come for dinner tomorrow evening?" she asked. Your grandmother and great-aunt Winnifred will be here, and they want to see you and meet Connie."

"I'm sure that will be fine," Greg said. "I'll call if it's a problem for Connie." He worked the remainder of the day catching up on paperwork.

He was surprised by a visit from Sheriff Fowler around 2:30 p.m. Adam Fowler knocked, and then entered without waiting for permission. He tossed a file onto Greg's desk and stood waiting while Greg scanned it.

Greg whistled when he read the report on the tire tracks taken from the woods the night of Connie's prowler incident. Looking up, he said, "I was so sure the tire tracks would be the same as the ones from the accident scene. I can't believe the two incidences are unrelated."

"Neither can I," Fowler said. "The tracks are similar. They evidently are from the same type of tires, but not the same tires. Our perpetrator was apparently driving a different vehicle when he decided to visit Miss Mitchell at home. I've got a man calling the dealerships in the surrounding area looking for our suspect vehicle. So far he's come up with very little. I'm assigning someone to stay with Erin when she comes home from the hospital on Friday. Security at the hospital is keeping an eye on her until then. If our man thinks she might be able to identify him, he might just try something once she comes home. I'm not taking any chances. Can you think of anyone who might be willing to do a little double duty for a few days?"

Greg immediately thought of Mike. "I think Deputy Cook would probably be the right man for the job. We've been working closely on this case, and I'm sure he wants to help see it through."

Fowler nodded. "Let Mike know about the change in the duty roster, okay? He stood up and left, leaving Greg deep in thought. He decided to check with the rental car companies in the area about the second vehicle.

He gave up after an hour. No one remembered renting a Lincoln to anyone fitting the description of the suspect in the last two weeks. Frustrated, he dug out the report from the accident scene. There had to be a link between the two cars. He was sure of it.

Reading the report, he remembered the paint sample taken from the bumper of Connie's car. Perhaps the second car was a loaner from a dealership. It made sense that the suspect would want to have the damage repaired as soon as possible. If he were wealthy enough to drive a brand new Lincoln, he would surely demand another car of similar quality to use while his was being repaired. Taking out the phone books, he started making calls again.

He'd had no luck and decided to call it a day at five. He was meeting Connie at her house for dinner and would be staying the night again. It wasn't that he didn't trust the other deputies, he just felt that it was his job to keep her safe when he could.

He stopped off at home to pack a change of clothes.

Forty-one

It had been a bad week. He hadn't been able to get close to his quarry. The cops always seemed to be around her. He wondered how much she knew. He tried to get to the Sims woman at the hospital, but the presence of the security guards botched his plan.

He knew she'd regained consciousness because he loitered around the desk listening for information before trying to see her. Her recovery was apparently big news. The nurses talked of little else that day while he was there. She was expected to make a full recovery. That didn't please him! Of his loving wife, there was still no sign.

The house was starting to smell now. The remains of two weeks worth of half-eaten meals and dirty dishes filled the kitchen, and the garbage was overflowing. He stayed away as much as possible. Cleaning wasn't his job. He'd picked the car up on Friday. It looked as good as new. He'd told the dealership to send the bill to his wife. They didn't question him about that.

On Wednesday, the newspaper carried a follow-up story on the murder of Eleanor Lincoln. Sheriff Fowler was quoted as saying, "We're closing in on the killer." He went on to say that new evidence would make an arrest imminent.

That scared him. He needed to finish this thing soon. Without that Mitchell woman, there would be nothing to tie him to the crime scene. He threw the paper into the wastebasket in his office and decided to go home.

She let herself into the house quietly. She was fairly certain he wasn't at home. The car wasn't parked in the drive or the garage. She didn't want any trouble today. She just needed a few things from her room and then she would be gone. She noticed the awful smell as soon as she stepped into the foyer. She wrinkled her nose in distaste. Hearing something crunch underfoot, she looked down.

The floor was littered with broken glass from the console mirror. Stepping into the living room, she saw the torn papers littering the floor. Stooping, she picked up a few small pieces. She was not surprised to find that they belonged to the divorce papers. She'd always known he had a temper.

Going into the kitchen, she looked at the mess he'd made there. No wonder the house smelled so bad. She guessed she'd better call someone to come in and clean before she returned home. By then, she hoped he would be gone. Her attorney had assured her that there would be no problem getting him out of the house. She hoped that was true.

She went upstairs to her room. It looked undisturbed. Evidently he'd not been in here since she'd left. She gathered the things she needed and packed them into the overnight bag from the closet. She stood still and looked around the room. She only needed to gather her jewelry, and she would be done. She sighed sadly and walked to the vanity.

He saw her car parked in the driveway when he arrived home. All the rage he'd been feeling erupted, and he took the gun from the glove compartment in the car and entered the house. He stole quietly upstairs. He could hear sounds coming from her room. He watched from the hallway as she packed her bag. When she went to the vanity, he stepped into the room. She was too busy sorting through her jewelry to notice him. She turned then. Shaking with anger, he lifted the gun and fired.

She saw his reflection in the mirror, saw the gun he held. She turned, horrified. The sound of the gunshot echoed loudly in her ears. She looked down at the crimson stain spreading across the front of her white sweater.

She sank to the floor. The pain was tearing across her chest now, making her gasp for breath. She heard footsteps crossing the hardwood floor and looking up, she saw her husband standing over her. His face was contorted with rage.

She was lying on the floor now, her sweater covered in blood. Her eyes were still open as he stared down at her. They were pleading for help, but his eyes were cold and empty. She closed her eyes as he raised the gun one again.

He left her lying in a pool of blood as he ransacked her room. Taking the jewelry and the money from her purse, he went to his own room. He packed his suitcases quickly, leaving little behind. With the jewelry he had taken and the money he'd invested in his own name for the last ten years, he would be fine.

It wouldn't be what he had become used to, but he was certain there was another woman, with even more money than his late unlamented wife, waiting for him somewhere. With his charm and talent, he would soon be sitting pretty again. This time he would make sure he controlled the money and the woman.

It was a shame the thing had gotten so out of hand, but all things considered, maybe it was for the best. He'd grown very tired of his life as of late. It was time to move on from here. The events of the last month had merely precipitated it.

He drove slowly out of town, careful not to attract any unwanted attention. He was sorry he would be unable to take care of the Sims woman, but it wasn't as if she could identify him as the one who'd run her off the road. Unfortunately, the other one *could* place him at the scene of a crime. She was a loose end he couldn't afford to leave.

He was sorry he'd given into the impulse to kill his wife. It complicated things a bit, but not too much. She had left him little choice. He really couldn't afford to have her lawyer poking his nose through their records of the last ten years. Too many things wouldn't have added up correctly.

He would never have been allowed to keep the money he'd taken. At least this way the money would still be his. He would have to leave the country when he was done, but he'd always wanted to live abroad anyway. He was sure it would be days before the body was found.

Her family knew she hadn't been living at home these last two weeks, and he was sure they would know she'd been planning to leave. He assumed she'd been packing for a trip. She always kept her sister and her parents informed when she was going to be gone. Yes, he was certain it would be days before anyone searched the house looking for her. If he were lucky, it would be weeks. If things went well, it would soon be finished, and he would be on his way to a new life.

He checked into a cheap motel just off the interstate under an assumed name. He paid cash for a two-day stay, and the clerk handed him the room key without any questions. The room was sleazy-looking and not quite clean. He didn't care. It suited his purpose at the moment and was close to where he wanted to be. CR 358 was just five minutes away from her. It was perfect. Lying down on the lumpy mattress, he fell asleep.

Forty-two

Connie was pleasantly surprised when Greg showed up at school around 3:30. She was pleased, too, with the invitation to dinner. She was glad she'd worn the new emerald green skirt to school that day. Greg had to work until five, so Connie stayed at the station grading some papers in his office.

Greg strolled into the office around 5:15 just as she was finishing up the last of the papers. She gathered her things, and they walked to his car. The temperature had dropped during the afternoon, and there was a biting wind blowing. The snow started as they arrived in Blue Springs. It was falling rather heavily by the time they arrived at the Reed's.

They darted from the car and ran under cover of the small porch. Carol Reed opened the door before Greg could knock. She looked very pleased to see both of them. She ushered them into the living room. She offered them each a sherry, and then Connie was introduced to Greg's grandmother and his great-aunt Winnifred. Grandmother Dorothy was petite like Patricia, with snapping green eyes and snow-white hair. She hugged Greg warmly and then Connie as well. With laughter in her eyes, she said to Greg, "It's about time you considered giving me a granddaughter and some great grandchildren as well."

Greg didn't seem surprised by her remarks. He laughed and remarked, "Glad you're happy, Grandmother."

Grant-Aunt Winnifred was a younger version of her mother. She was quiet, though, like Carron. Her hair was a beautiful silvery gray, and her eyes were dark brown. She had little to say, but seemed happy nonetheless.

Dinner was a happy affair. Afterwards, they sat talking for a while. Back in the living room, Connie stood before the fireplace gazing at the pictures on the mantel. Greg's father joined her there. He gave names to the faces in the photographs that she didn't recognize.

The last picture on the mantel was of a group of men dressed in suits. Mr. Reed said, "These are the associates and partners from my firm. It was taken about ten years ago. Most of the men are still with me. A few have moved on to greener pastures, though."

Connie perused the picture. She was able to easily identify James and John. She was surprised to see Greg in the picture, too. They began discussing Greg's law career, and her attention was diverted from the picture. Noting her look, Mr. Reed commented, "I guess my son didn't bother to tell you that he has a law degree, as well as one in criminology."

"No, he didn't," Connie replied.

"He worked with me for about three years, and then decided he was more suited to police work. He was right. He was a good attorney, but his passion is law enforcement," James said. He placed the picture back on the mantle, and the conversation turned to other things. Later, Connie and Greg sat alone in the living room. The Reeds had left to take Greg's grandmother and his great-aunt home. The firelight cast a soft glow around the room and Connie was content to sit quietly beside Greg, their hands entwined. The ringing of Greg's cell phone shattered the peace of the moment. Greg sighed heavily and reached for the phone.

Forty-three

Connie sat in the living room waiting for Deputy Crawford to drive her home. Greg had been visibly upset by the phone call he had received and left immediately, after a quick call to the station to arrange for another deputy to come for her. Connie hadn't wanted to pry, and he hadn't offered any explanation as to the nature of the call. Connie had assured him that she didn't mind waiting alone for her ride home.

Connie stood and wandered back to look at the pictures on the mantel. She picked up the photo from the law firm and studied Greg, admiring the way he stood so proudly with his co-workers. Her eyes moved on to the others in the picture, then suddenly stopped.

The dark-haired man standing near Mr. Reed gave her an agonizing jolt. He was younger, and the hair was different, but that smile was all too familiar. She felt herself pale, and she stumbled back from the mantel in shock. "Oh dear God, that's him," whispered hoarsely.

Forty-four

It was dark now and very quiet. He parked his car just up the road from her house. He was careful to pull far off the road where he would not easily be seen. He tucked the gun into the waistband of his dark pants and pulled the hood of the jacket over his head. He slipped into the woods and crept slowly through the underbrush.

It was bitterly cold now, and his breath made little whorls of white in the air. He was panting when he came to the clearing behind the house. He stood watching for a long time. The windows of the house were dark, and he could see no cars in the drive. He waited, searching for any signs of activity in or near the house. He checked his watch. It was nearly 9 p.m.

He stole slowly through the yard and onto the porch. He fumbled with the lock. It refused to give. Cursing under his breath, he left the porch and went around to the back of the house. He would have to get in another way.

The screen was loose on one of the windows, and he was able to remove it with ease. The lock on the window was more difficult. It took him a full ten minutes before it gave way. It groaned as he pushed it up. He jumped back, startled. He waited with bated breath for sounds from inside. There were none.

Relieved, he opened the window fully and climbed through it. The small flashlight allowed him to see better what he needed to do. He replaced the window screen and closed the window. He searched the house looking for the best place to hide. He decided on the closet in the master bedroom. Pushing the clothes aside, he was able to slip in easily. He pulled the clothes back into place and settled in to wait.

Forty-five

She was unsure just how long she had been lying on the cold, hard floor. She was numb with cold and fear. Her chest hurt, and her head felt as if it had been split in two, but she...

She remembered everything clearly. His eyes had been so cold. His face had born no trace of the man she had loved. It had been a face filled with hate.

She had closed her eyes trying to blot out the ugliness and the pain. He hadn't cared. He had shot her again without hesitation. She had lain very still and listened as he had ransacked the room and taken her things.

She could feel the blood running down from her head and into her eyes. Perhaps it was all the blood that had made him assume she was dead. He had left her lying there, but she could hear him in his own room. When she heard him go downstairs and out the door, she tried crawling to the phone beside her bed. The movement caused her to lapse into unconsciousness.

She listened now for some sound that might indicate his return. It was quiet, too quiet. There was no one here to help her. She would have to help herself. She struggled to turn. She slid on the blood-soaked floor as she crawled to the phone. It slid from her bloody fingers twice before she was able to punch the emergency 911 button.

It was becoming more difficult to breathe, and she was barely able to hear the voice of the operator. She was unable to respond to the questions. She could only gasp for air and hope that they would send help. She dropped the phone for the last time and felt herself slipping into the black void of death.

Forty-six

Connie sat quietly on the long ride home, her mind filled with questions and her body numb with fear. Deputy Crawford didn't even attempt to engage her in conversation. His trained eyes took in her pale face and trembling hands. Whatever had happened back at the Reed's had shaken her up very badly. Greg had called dispatch and asked them to send a car for her. He had been just finishing up his rounds then and offered to go. He knew Sheriff Fowler would have wanted it that way.

Greg was already gone by the time he arrived in Blue Springs, and Connie wasn't in any shape to give information. He wondered again what had happened to send Greg back into town without his fiancée. Everyone in the department knew what had been going on with them. They also knew Greg seldom let her out of his sight these days.

He pulled into the drive at Connie's house and killed the engine. She didn't wait for him to help her from the car. She was at the door, fumbling with the lock, when he came onto the porch. The door refused to budge, and she was forced to let him try. He shoved hard and nearly fell into the room when the door gave way.

He straightened up awkwardly and gave Connie a sheepish look. She managed a weak smile at his obvious embarrassment.

He made a quick search of the house as he had been instructed. Seeing nothing amiss, he bade Connie goodnight and returned to his car.

He called in to dispatch and gave his location and a brief report. All he needed to do now was wait for Greg to return, and he could go home. He settled in for the wait. It was cold in the car, and he considered going back inside. Miss Mitchell was nice, and he was certain she wouldn't mind. He was about to step onto the porch when the lights went out in the front of the house. He shrugged and, retracing his steps, got back into the cold car. He pulled his jacket up around his ears and settled deep into the seat.

Forty-seven

Greg drove swiftly, his mind racing as well. He was thankful that Connie hadn't pressed for details.

The house on Wisteria Drive was awash with emergency personnel when Greg arrived. He parked the car haphazardly and raced across the lawn and into the house. He stepped over the threshold and carefully avoided the broken glass that littered the floor. Adam Fowler beckoned to him from the landing on the second floor. He climbed the stairs slowly, not really wanting to reach the top. He followed Adam into the nearest bedroom.

The grisly scene that met his eyes made his stomach turn. The bedroom was in complete disarray. Blood soaked the oak floor near the vanity and was spread across the room. The phone lying on the floor was covered with blood as well. He remembered too well how the body of Eleanor Lincoln had looked, covered in blood. He turned to Adam.

"Where is she?" he asked harshly.

Adam put his hand on Greg's shoulder before replying. "They've taken her to the hospital. They don't expect her to live through the night. Either one of her injuries should have been fatal. It's nothing short of a miracle that she was able to phone for help. The husband shot her twice, once in the chest and a second time in the head. We found divorce papers downstairs torn into pieces. Probably that's the reason for the shooting."

Greg said nothing. He merely turned and left. He left the house and drove to the hospital, making a few calls on the way. At the hospital, he was told that she was in surgery. He waited impatiently for the others to arrive.

Adam watched Greg leave. The crime scene had made him feel like retching as well. He wasn't used to this degree of violence. Shaking his head, he went back downstairs to wait while the rest of his team finished gathering evidence. He wondered where the husband was now. He was sure Greg would be out looking for him as soon as he was able.

Sheriff Fowler shook his head, trying to clear his thoughts. He was getting too old for this job. It was time to think about retiring.

Forty-eight

Connie locked the front door behind the deputy and went to the kitchen for a drink of water. How quickly the evening had turned ugly. The face in the picture had been a shocking reminder of the tragic events of these last weeks. She trembled as she remembered that face with those empty, arctic eyes.

She needed to talk to Greg, needed to tell him about the picture. But, most of all, she needed him to hold her tightly and tell her that everything would be fine. She wanted so badly to pick up the phone and dial his number, but she didn't. The call he had received must have been urgent or he would never have left her. She knew he would come to her as soon as he could. She took a deep breath to calm herself, then turned out the living room lights and went to her room.

She undressed quickly and went to the bathroom to shower and brush her teeth. She still couldn't get the face in the picture out of her mind. Who was he, and what was he doing in a picture with Greg and his father? She prayed that Greg would come soon so that she could ask him.

He listened from his hiding place in the closet as she fumbled around in the bedroom. When he heard the water running in the bathroom, he slipped quietly from the closet. He looked carefully around, making sure the cop was nowhere in the house. Back in the bedroom, he stepped into the closet once more. He would wait until she was asleep to make his move.

Her shower completed, Connie brushed her teeth and returned to her room. The hot shower had failed to stop the shivers that racked her body. She climbed wearily under the covers and reached for her Rosary on the bedside table. She found it hard to concentrate. Her mind continually wandered, and she gave up trying to pray. She lay in bed and listened for the sound of Greg's car. Exhaustion overtook her, and she finally slipped into a troubled sleep.

Outside, Deputy Crawford huddled deeper into his jacket, and hoped Greg would return soon.

Forty-nine

He stole silently from the closet and stood at the foot of her bed, listening to her deep, even breathing. The moonlight, streaming through the window, played across her face. His expression was hard and his eyes cold as he surveyed her. Slipping the gun from his waistband, he walked to the side of the bed. He sat down next to her. She frowned in her sleep and rolled away from him. He put the gun to her temple and called her name.

Connie thought she was dreaming again. The voice calling her name was ugly and threatening. She struggled to get away from it. She felt the cold steel of the gun barrel pressed to her head and opened her eyes. The man seated on her bed was her nightmare come to life. She started to scream, but he slapped her hard across the face. Completely aware now, she watched in horror as he raised his hand again.

He stroked the side of her face where he had slapped her just minutes before. She recoiled from his touch and he laughed sardonically. He grabbed a handful of her hair and pulled her closer to him. Trembling, she prayed for help.

He began to speak, and she listened in utter bewilderment at the poison spilling from his lips. He spoke of Eleanor as if she had been nothing more than a toy, to be played with and discarded when she grew boring. He was even more hateful when he spoke of his wife. Connie grew colder when he described how he had taken her life earlier that day.

He ranted and raved about her interference in his plans. She was aghast when he spoke of Erin's accident. It was then that Connie realized she'd been hoping all along that Greg had been wrong about the accident.

She tried to pull away once more, but he held tightly to her hair. He laughed, watching her futile struggles. He was enjoying her obvious panic. Connie's mind was racing frantically, searching for a way to break free. Screaming would do no good. The deputy outside would never hear her, and she didn't want to antagonize her tormentor again.

She was petrified with fear as she agonized over what to do. If only she could reach the lamp beside the bed. Trying to distract him she went limp, praying he would loosen his hold. He did. She grabbed blindly for the lamp and swung it with all her might at his head. It connected with a dull thud. He fell to the floor, bleeding profusely.

Connie scrambled across the bed and raced for the door. She heard him moan, and the sound lent wings to her feet as she raced across the cold floor. At the front door, she yanked the deadbolt back and tried to open the door.

It wouldn't budge. Panic-stricken and sobbing, she tried again. Hearing movement from the bedroom, she gave up and hurried to the kitchen. She was slipping out the door when she felt his hand grab at her shoulder. Screaming, she slid through the opening and ran across the yard.

He pursued her as he had in her dream. She knew she would never make it to Deputy Crawford. Without hesitation, she turned towards the woods. Her feet were quickly becoming numb with cold, and her breathing was labored.

She ran as swiftly as she could, ducking under the cover of the tall trees at the edge of the woods. Pausing to catch her breath, she listened for footsteps. What she heard was a gunshot. It reverberated through the cold, frozen air with deadly intention. Biting back a sob, she raced on again. *Dear Lord*, she prayed, *please protect me.*

Fifty

Deputy Crawford rubbed his cold hands together and blew on them. His fingers were numb with cold, and his legs weren't much better. He decided to try and awaken Connie. Opening the car door, he was startled by the sound of screaming. Drawing his gun from the holster, he ran across the yard.

The screaming had stopped, but he was certain it had come from the back of the house. Stealthily, he crept around the house. The sight of Connie fleeing across the yard alarmed him.

He never heard the footsteps behind him, he only felt the impact as he was knocked to the ground. The gun flew from his cold fingers, and he lay helpless. The man standing over him laughed and then fired.

Fifty-one

Lights flashing, Greg sped through the night. He wanted to get to Connie. He needed to be with her now. He needed the comfort of her arms and the warmth of her smile. The ordeal at the hospital was behind him now. It had been rough. She was going to live, but it would be a long, tough road to a complete recovery. She would make it though; the prognosis was good. He wondered what had driven her husband, a successful, wealthy man, to attempt murder. He would know soon enough.

CR 358 was as dark as always, and Greg was grateful for the powerful, high beams on the squad car. He had left his own car at the station after leaving the hospital. Once he had seen Connie, he would begin his search for the suspect in tonight's shooting. Rosemount was a small town. It would be hard to hide for long.

He raced on, the powerful engine eating up the miles. He slowed as he neared the drive and prepared to pull in behind the parked squad car. He was alarmed to see the driver's door standing open. Killing the engine, he jumped from his car. Seeing nothing, he ran to the front porch. Pounding on the door, he waited for Connie to open it. He waited just a few seconds before applying his shoulder to the recalcitrant door.

Inside, he heard nothing. He called to Connie, but there was no response. A cold chill permeated the house as if someone had left a window or door open. Worried, he ran down the hallway and into her room. He flipped on the light, saw the broken lamp and the dark stains on the floor by the bed.

Sweating now, he raced through the house calling her name. She wasn't anywhere in the house. There was more blood on the floor in the kitchen, and the door was standing open. He hurried out, still calling. He stopped short at the sight of Deputy Crawford lying on the cold ground. Bending down, he felt for a pulse. He was still alive.

Deputy Crawford opened his eyes and struggled to tell Greg what had happened. His thoughts were muddled, and his vision cloudy. He could only point in the direction in which he had seen Connie running.

After calling for help with the phone attached to his belt, Greg took off in the direction Crawford had indicated. He prayed he wouldn't be too late.

Fifty-two

Deep in the woods, Connie huddled beneath a stand of cedar trees, trying to catch her breath. She could hear her pursuer stumbling through the woods nearby. He was coming closer now, and she quelled the urge to run. Crouching, she waited quietly as he passed close to the spot where she was hidden. She could hear him cursing as he beat at the branches that tore at his clothes.

She waited for a few minutes more before leaving the relative safety of her hiding place. She was going to try and circle back towards the house. It was the only place to call for help. She offered a silent, thankful prayer to her grandfather in heaven for teaching her about these woods.

She collected her thoughts and then started her stealthy trek back to the house. Her frozen feet made walking difficult. She stumbled often, falling several times. Her silent litany of prayers gave comfort as she struggled to remain calm.

Beating his way through the woods, cursing loudly, he vented his anger at Connie. When he caught her, he would kill her quickly. He was in no mood to toy with her now. He wanted to be gone from this place and all its trouble. The blood from the wound on his head had congealed in the cold air, so it no longer dripped down his face.

He paused for a moment listening for any sound that might betray her location. At first he heard nothing, then a soft thud and a scurrying sound that echoed on the frosty night air. Dismayed, he realized the sound was coming from behind him. She was trying to get back to the house. Even angrier now, knowing that he had been fooled, he hurriedly turned and retraced his steps.

Greg moved as swiftly and as quietly as he could through the dense woods. He remembered all the times he and Connie had walked these woods hand-in-hand. It made it easier now to move quietly. It was silent in the woods, save for the sounds of the night animals. The owls hooted in the trees, and he could hear the raccoons scurrying to get out of the way as he moved nimbly forward. He listened for other sounds, but heard nothing.

He kept on, tracking into the deep woods, the powerful flashlight lighting his way. He stopped short once, seeing signs of disturbance in the undergrowth near a stand of cedars.

Someone had been here recently, of that he was sure. There were fresh tracks through the dead leaves that carpeted the earth. Moving slower now, he trained the beam of the light downward, looking for other clues. Suddenly he heard a thud, and then nothing more. He hurried on heedless of the noise he was making, fear driving him. *What if he was too late?*

Connie stumbled and fell once again. Trying to regain her footing, she slipped a second time in the wet leaves that lay on the ground. Exhausted, she lay there for a few precious moments, gathering strength. She heard running footsteps and tried to get up. Her frozen feet refused to obey her command. She dragged herself forward slowly, praying all the while.

Fifty-three

He came upon her suddenly. He watched in silence as she pulled herself across the cold, damp floor of the forest. He laughed knowing she was his now. She wasn't going to be able to get away this time. She was like a deer caught in the headlights. Her eyes were wide and frightened as she lay on the ground.

He moved forward swiftly and was upon her. He rolled her over with his foot and kicked her. She tried to kick back, but her legs were leaden and refused to move. She began screaming and flailing her arms when he kicked her again. He aimed the gun at her head and pulled back on the trigger.

When Greg heard Connie screaming, he threw caution to the winds and raced on toward the sound. What he saw sent fear down his spine. The killer was standing over her with the gun pointed downward, his finger on the trigger. Fearful of using his own weapon, he charged forward and knocked him to the ground.

Greg felt the body under his go limp and looked down dazed. He found the flashlight and shone it down on the attacker. He was lying awkwardly, his head resting on a large rock. Blood ran onto the ground and soaked into the leaves. Leaning down, he checked for a pulse. He drew back aghast when he recognized the face of the man lying dead at his feet.

Fifty-four

Robert Westlake's empty eyes gazed up into the frigid, black night. His sister's husband was dead. Greg turned away, feeling sick. There was nothing more to be done. He wondered again how it had come to this. He had never suspected that his brother-in-law could be capable of such evil. He walked away from the body.

Connie lay trembling with cold and shock; her eyes dry, her voice silent. Bending down, he picked her up gently and walked away, back through the forest. She never uttered a sound. He held her close, trying to warm her with his own body heat.

Back at the house, she was cold and still as they loaded her into the rescue unit. She was silent even then. On the long ride to the hospital, he sat beside her holding her hand and stroking her hair. Her eyes were vacant, and her grip slack. He prayed as he had never prayed before.

Fifty-five

Sitting beside her bed, he held tightly to her hand. She looked small and lost in the stark hospital bed. Her eyes were closed now; she was sleeping. The injection she had been given had induced the deep sleep.

His throat tightened as he remembered the horror on his parents' face when he had told them of the shooting. It had been far worse when he'd had to tell them of Robert's perfidy. They had aged before his eyes. Like him, they had never suspected the wickedness that lay beneath the thin veneer of charm that was their son-in-law.

Thinking back over the events of the past several hours made him angry. He was angry with himself. Why hadn't he connected Connie's suspect with his brother-in-law? He supposed because he had never paid him much attention. He'd never spent much time with him, and Robert had absented himself from most family gatherings for the past ten years. He hadn't really known his brother-in-law at all.

He had certainly not known of the throat surgery that Robert had undergone a year ago. His mother had told him about that when he had mentioned that it was Robert's voice that Connie had noticed first. Robert had had several growths removed from his larynx. The resulting hoarseness had not healed. It was especially apparent when he raised his voice. Greg realized he probably hadn't even seen Robert three times in the last year.

If only he had known...he could have saved Connie and Carron from the pain and anguish they were both suffering now. Only Connie was unaware of whom her attacker was. Perhaps it was for the best. There would be time later to tell her. He rested his head on the bed and closed his eyes.

Fifty-six

Connie awakened around ten the following morning. She barely remembered the events of the previous evening. In the coming days, she would recapture and relive those moments many times. Greg was by her side as much as possible. Connie had been appalled to learn the identity of the killer. She wept tears of sorrow for Carron, Greg, and the rest of his family. They were so guilt-ridden for never suspecting the anguish that Carron kept hidden too well. Carron continued to recover, but her eyes were deep wells of pain, and she seldom smiled. It was a dismal time for everyone.

In January, Carron left for an extended visit to Florida to stay with her longtime friend Kathryn Scott. Deputy Crawford had recovered as well and returned to work the first of the year. Sheriff Fowler announced that he would be retiring that year and asked Greg to consider running for sheriff. Greg agreed.

Carron returned in April, still quiet, but more like her old self. She threw herself into helping Connie and Greg plan their wedding. Connie's nightmares had subsided and she, too, returned to work. She would finish out the year, but it would be her last for some time. She and Greg were to be married in June and planned to start a family immediately.

They met often with Father Murphy and sought his guidance. They completed the required classes and worked on Greg's campaign.

Epilogue

On the third Saturday in June, Connie walked down the aisle with Mr. Sims at her side. She wore her grandmother's wedding dress and her mother's pearls. She was radiantly happy.

At the front of the church, Mr. Sims beamed down at her and kissed her soundly before handing her over to Greg. Greg, tall and solemn in his black tuxedo, took her hand and they turned to the altar.

The lovely ceremony brought tears to Connie's eyes as she gazed in wonder around the old church. The small church was filled to capacity with family and friends. Late afternoon sunlight filtered through the stained glass windows, and danced on the pews and across the altar, with a myriad of rainbow colors. White roses filled the church, and their fragrant perfume lingered in the air.

Erin stood by her side as her maid of honor. Her hair had grown back and was curled becomingly around her face. Erin grew misty eyed as she realized that she, too, would soon be standing at this very same altar. Mike had proposed yesterday. She hadn't hesitated to accept. Her love for him had grown quickly, and she was hard-pressed to remember what it had been like without him. She watched as Greg slipped the ring onto Connie's finger and smiled at the love she could see in both their eyes. It would be a wonderful marriage.

Greg was thinking those same thoughts. The woman standing beside him was his wife. For better or worse, they were joined forever. In his heart, he knew it would always be for better. There would be hard times. They would conquer them together.

He squeezed her hand, and she looked up at him. She smiled a gentle smile that filled her eyes and his heart. Father Murphy pronounced them husband and wife, and Greg tilted his head and kissed her soundly. As he gazed into her eyes, brilliant with the love she felt for him, he knew, she had come out of her dreams and into his.

Meet Anita Lourcey Tooke

Anita is a full time homemaker and lives in north Florida with her husband and daughter. An avid reader, she had always wanted to write a book. Out Of Her Dreams is her first book. She is currently working on her second.

Look For These Other Titles

From

Wings ePress, Inc.

Romance Novels

Double Moon Destiny by *lizzie starr
Love Through A Stranger's Eyes by Jan Springer
Michael; A Gift of Trust by Margaret B. Lawrence
Out Of Her Dreams by Anita Lourcey Tooke
The Reluctant Landlord by Susanne Marie Knight

General Fiction Novels

Lost Almost by Lynnette Baughman
Deadly Diamonds by Judith R. Parker

Coming In September 2002

A Change Of Plans by Ann B. Morris
A Deadly Agent by Sue Sweet
Designing Heart by Patricia Prendergast
Heroes And Hunks by Christine Poe
Lately Of England by Sara V. Olds and Roberta O. Major
Keeper Of The Singing Bones by Marilyn Gardiner
Secrets by Judi Phillips

General Fiction Novels

Endless Place by William J. Calabrese

Be sure to visit us at http://www.wings-press.com
for a complete listing of our available and upcoming titles.